THE TEST

*Also by John Fraser and published by
AESOP Modern Fiction:*

Animal Tales
Behaving Well
Best Friends
Black Masks
Blue Light / Starting Over
The Case
Confessions
The Cure
Down from the Stars
The Ends of the Earth
Enterprising Women
Exploring the Clouds
Fake Fur
The Future's Coming Everywhere
Happy Always
Hard Places
An Illusion of Sun
The Magnificent Wurlitzer
Medusa
Military Roads
The Observatory
The Other Shore
People You Will Never Meet
The Red Bird
The Red Tank
Runners
'S'
Short Lives
Sisters
Soft Landing
The Storm
Strangers and Refugees
Thinking Scientifically
Thirty Years
Three Beauties
Tomorrow the Victory
Unsteady States, Vol. I
Wayfaring
Wisdom

THE TEST

John Fraser

AESOP Modern Fiction
Oxford

AESOP Modern Fiction
An imprint of AESOP Publications
Martin Noble Editorial / AESOP
28a Abberbury Road, Oxford OX4 4ES, UK
www.aesopbooks.com

First edition published by AESOP Publications

www.johnfraserfiction.com

A catalogue record of this book is available from the British Library.

First edition 2022, revised 2024

ISBN: 978-1-914938-08-5

CONTENTS

THE TEST

THEY'RE SITTING in a danger zone – they're used to it. It's trite to say that everywhere is dangerous – it's true, but false as well. They sit quite close, but in their heads, they're indifferent to one another, and they both hope – 'this is an illusion, a place that disappears', part of their stories that will be cancelled, memory kicking in and out what you don't want.

They plan a future.

'Nature rampaging on the islands, everywhere else cemented over,' Ahmad says. 'It's a good remedy. It shows – we aren't just idiots. We can modify where we are – that's what we do.'

'There's other questions,' says Noura. 'Me, for instance. I love being alone, isolated, in solitude. You can't be – unless it's for a bet. Everybody is watched, replaceable, tested. Each person has their squad, their backing, colleagues who envy and record. Families who count you like you're on their hand – a finger.'

'They say everything written, passed on,' says Ahmad. 'Should be an act of political resistance – unless, I suppose, you're on the other side, *an* other side. We've had this one out before: "commitment". No one understands it now, unless they were there, or read the history. The history is always more interesting anyway – but it's gone. Not there, not anywhere; to resist.'

'I know being with me makes you suffer,' Noura says, not telling Ahmad how he's missed the point and not wanting to follow the argument herself – 'You just need say.'

There's a slide of shale beside them. There are lots, so many – they don't want to move. They aren't being logical.

She says, 'Would writing include graffiti? And resignations? Love letters and dear johns? Orders of the day – menus and rules of engagement? Only profs read other profs nowadays – most people only read their friends.'

'In some countries, poetry counts much more than here,' says Ahmad.

'They're always burning, down there,' Noura says, peering down at the ochre village, its ochre plots. 'Halms, or thatch – in the fall, when the thatch is full of larvae, insects of all types ... up it goes. On with a new roof.'

Patches of smoke go looking for their lookalikes, join up, make a dark low cloud.

'People come here when there's trouble, to do good. Some to be good. Then, there's those who want to do and be: saints. We're near the top of the slope,' says Ahmad. 'We could go up to the ridge, over – and leave the fighting and the feeding to the other guys, the ones who seek a beginning, or an end. The self-fulfilling.'

'The boys on the other side bring their guns and shoot,' says Noura. 'Those trail-bikes! All wild! And what if they rape me? What would you do then?'

'Not much,' says Ahmad. 'I'm useless in such situations. Besides, there is no protocol. I run when everybody runs, and if someone doesn't run, it's too bad for them.'

'Exactly,' Noura says. 'When we left home, we should have gone straight on. Instead we took a left, and down the hill, they're Buddhists, they have anger management from their birth. Anger and management – it isn't wanted, it gets you nowhere. But we've got no context, no one is interested, no one feels a duty – not of any kind, except maybe to those gold statues. I hate this place, and the place we left, and the journey was shit too. I'm not used to all the drinking and fighting. I'd like to meet good people who aren't peaceful with it....'

And they laugh, but not so much.

'There was war, remember, when we left,' says Ahmad, 'And from the start we were on the losing side, us, the good guys. I had no choice, I was well-known for being good.'

Noura laughs, she says, 'I should have stayed. I thought I'd be safer out – but for a while; then going back.'

'You know I'm a coward,' Ahmad says. 'So – I brought a pistol. It only kills one at a time. It's archaic – you'll have seen it in the movies. It sticks out, digs in, so you can't sit. It's your libido, always rampant, always urging on. What would a rifle do, I wonder?' And he laughs.

'Let's get a bonze to bless us,' Noura says. 'Perhaps they sell armour too.'

*

The Black Sea,' Ahmad says, 'was called that because of the dark fogs. Now, it's oil. My family went there before the dictatorships

– I have photos of them, happy as seals. The men, naked like the Russians, like the tsars. A fiasco – my cousins, free and fresh of face, unveiled, or wearing a niqab and nothing more, or covered in cake deco – sugar roses and peonies....'

'In memory,' says Noura, 'we're all romantics – think of Goethe, displaced by three wars, in a tent for decades, crawling with cholera and buboes. Schiller too, backing the wrong side, and Marx with his flintlock, on the barricades; Munich, the revolutionary city....'

'You're a compendium, Noura,' Ahmad says, 'when you're not a thesaurus. If you were an emporium, we could get something on a bun. Fried things: dripping, at the least.'

'Being chased out, bombed and martyred – it's part of life's cycle,' Noura says. 'A rite. Don't think about it when it happens, but take notes to compare, when you are out and a celebrity.'

'I understand why everybody does what they do,' says Ahmad. 'Understand – it's a killer. You lose everything you ought to be, what you are. We're free to wander round, looking in the windows of other people's houses. Not everybody suffers: if you're not poor, you're rich. If you don't lose, you win. If you don't believe lies – you know the truth.'

'Pelicans fly half-way round the world,' says Noura, 'Each year. Naked, just feathers. They know the world is round, they fly back with their kids; no one helps them, no one shoots them down. They're citizens of everywhere. Once, we would be asked in. Now, it's hard. The plan should be to stay until the last instant. If nothing happens, it's because you're doing nothing, knowing nothing.'

'Rich people leave,' says Ahmad. 'Some stay, if they've got big families. Most people, people who are poor, or getting so –

they stay – send out someone, maybe they'll be saved, maybe pull everybody out. But mostly – it's going on and struggling, and mostly waiting, clinging. If you're us, Noura, you understand, and you've lost everything. You're not a pelican, although you know the earth is round. The birds, up high, can see where to avoid, and where is flourishing. Even when everywhere is getting hot.'

*

'No,' says the bonze. 'It's not like that. You must bless yourselves. I'm nobody to you. You're not superstitious. Forget the statues.'

*

Ahmad scampers up the hill. There's shouting, shooting. What a celebration. Maybe not. He disappears – another one. It's life ... he had his chance, he took it, he was wrong. Noura cries – not for Ahmad, for herself. Ahmad was not Monsieur Bovary.

'When you see the tents,' says the kindly bonze, 'you can doss there ... and you must wait. There may be someone good around, it won't be you. You won't be, not again, you won't be good. Don't kick against it.'

'Oh no!' thinks Noura. 'There's been so many tales like this – displacement, loss of this and that, reunifications, but with people who are strangers now....'

She has dollars, sewn in. She gets out of there. No politics involved.

She starts again.

*

'You can do hair, Noura,' the lady, Ekaterina, says. 'Anybody can. Learn the language, and about life too.'

'Long or short?' says Noura, grinning. Ekaterina must be into something *louche* – all those types, bosses of hair salons, are. Gangsters? Or prostitutes? Noura hopes it's tarts, no torture, not much vendetta.

'Where I came from,' Noura says, 'mother of all countries – prostitutes are mostly widows. God will avenge them. That's what people say.'

'Remember,' Ekaterina says, 'long or short. You can live here, Noura, sleep in the chair.'

It's a start, and starts don't last long.

The decisive step – like a puffin stepping off the cliff and into flight – to anywhere.... Ekaterina's boyfriend, Vladimir, gives Noura a promotion ... reception at his car-hire. 'Long or short?' Noura has to ask. Assimilation is complete!

'My problem is,' says Noura, 'lack of imagination.'

'No!' says Ekaterina, 'it's your gift. You left your home when war had finished. But you were right – peace is more deadly, quieter, and longer. Long or short – peace or war, you followed your best sense.'

'I know the world is round,' says Noura, 'and in the chair, when I'm asleep, I fly. My instinct works, but when I wake, there's only you and Vladimir, the chair – and endless guys who peek at me, mimic my 'long or short': and how they giggle! I'd rather be alone, and yet – the loneliness ...'

'Take photographs,' Ekaterina says. 'Your family, or someone else's – doesn't matter. Naked tsars or revolutionaries – what do you care? Then you can have them round you, thumb them, every night. You and your faith – there's no imagination there, it's frowned upon, and chivvied in the street....'

'Oh no,' says Noura, 'I've no faith in faith. I want ideas! Ahmad had lots, they did for him! What is my life? A brick in an invisible wall? A feather, dropped in flight and spiralling down, a wonder fast forgot? ... A drop of poison in the sea?'

The salon's windows are made bullet-proof.

'Remember each time to change the plates,' says Vladimir the boss. 'The motors should come back clean, but clients want a fresh start every time.'

'Like me,' thinks Noura. 'Unfortunately, I'm sane, and all the rest of them are not. I wish I could imagine things, like them. The horsemen and the dragon lady – they are loose upon the earth – maybe I'll be called on to make judgment, or more likely, it's already been decided, but there's not been time to write it down.... Bureaucracy, no doubt....'

'I know the war is over, Ekaterina,' Noura says aloud. 'But it wasn't proper war. There was fighting and soldiers, but a war has two sides. There, it was one, or many. No war, exactly. And now – I'm not in my genre. You told me – do everything straight, and by the book. I've always tried – the book I don't believe in, but it isn't necessary, you follow what it says. The book, any book, and then you can be yourself. But – here, there's no room, no time is left. It's flat again: my earth is flat!'

'You should see someone,' Ekaterina says.

'"Family happiness': we might have heard it all at bedtime,' Noura says. 'But we read from right to left. First came happiness, but the family came next and ended it. We had family, in a way – lots of makeshift beds, side by side, but the happiness was elusive.... More to the point was – '*a fundamental crisis of the object*'. It's out-of-date, from an age forgotten, like the gold-leaf electroscope – but what prescience! I might be able to get spare parts, for myself, since I am not an object any more. No one is ... we're all potential, like magnetism. Objects in every sense are on their sad way out.'

'It's a great idea,' Ekaterina says. 'A bit dusty, though. 'Spare parts' – not for yourself, of course, but selling them, installing if you have the means. Best aim for excitement: travelling without fuel.'

'Yes,' says Noura. 'Something, not nothing, but a something that won't fit into a paper bag.'

'Watch the paper bags, Noura,' says Vladimir, who's just come in. 'They all have your address. A line will form outside your door – except the door is ours!' And he laughs and laughs.

'Hair and hire, Noura,' Ekaterina says, quite sternly. 'Both require order. No random snip and clip. You rent the car, not a destination. You seem to have a speciality – it's chaos. You know, maybe you're a collector, connoisseur, of the aimless agonistic play of things. You see the universe as happenstance, with you – resigned. What order could you ask from a disorder? You don't sell anything – how can you choose who comes in your shop?'

'Chaos can't think, it has no mind – so, of course, it has an order,' Noura says. 'Thought and mind – they don't.'

Vladimir doffs his shapka to her. 'Well said, Noura,' he says, in mocking tones. 'An order has an origin, and every origin must have an end. Maybe you've found it, reached it. You should know!'

'It's true,' says Noura. 'I have seen frayed ends. And I have a little garden, a chaos garden, that I tend, and find an order there – or impose an order. Is it easy to impose an order, like you impose a chaos? How to tell the difference? It's like ends – they decay, they split, they seek arrays of different ends that would not be ends at all. Nor, I think, beginnings. I believe in free will and in destiny. I can't. No one can. I'm a miscreant, I believe in contradictories. But – if I can't, I don't.

'Can we save the world? Or lose ourselves? Has the last chance gone: and did it just slip away? Or did we make it go? Self murder, like poor Ahmad? That was free will and destiny. He didn't need believe in either, or to disbelieve....'

'Here's a secret, Noura,' says Vladimir, sliding a long arm round her, so that a thumb can flicker up and down her breast. 'I had in mind to save the world. And then I changed my mind. Modesty, and cowardice. A hard and dirty task left incomplete. Impossible, perhaps: or was it me?'

'You're not a good person, Vladimir,' says Noura. 'But you gave me work. Perhaps I should just save you, and let you off the hook of saving everyone.'

'No!' says Ekaterina. 'We take the risk that nothing that Noura says or what we do will make *us* change or make a change. Be very very careful, everyone!'

'I don't want that to be my risk too,' says Noura. 'But I want to keep the job.'

'How can you possibly believe in free will, silly?' Ekaterina asks Noura, and slaps Vladimir's hand. 'And you, Vladimir, in destiny?'

There's raids, of course. The cops, the gangsters ... which is worse, or best? The cops cut clients' pictures from their frames – 'O no!' says Noura. 'All those wigs! – our bigwig customers who've posed for snaps – postiches and quiffs, bangs and crops, longs, shorts, scorched earth and baobabs .... all to be done again.'

Of course, there's nothing to be found – and not Ekaterina, nor Vladimir. They weren't even hidden, just not there. Only Noura's there, and she's all over an illegal.

She's lucky – it's the gangsters find her.

'Don't bless me, friends,' she says. 'I'll do that for myself. As for torture and the rest – states do it better ... more equipment, more paid staff....'

So what? Noura's an intermediary, doesn't count. Not much, even for the state, for all its fuss.

She thinks, 'I must do something to be remembered by. What will that be? Does my mark count – or is that my proof of the universe being run by randomness? And yet, memory is not exactly random, though it comes fairly close.... I may be remembered involuntarily....'

*

Ekaterina needs her for the clean-up: she asks, 'Are you interested in the Wildlife Club, Noura?'

'I'm very close to animals,' Noura says, and sees Ekaterina has an eton-crop – it's easy, you can do it to yourself.

'Eton's a place where you can learn the tricks,' Ekaterina says. 'The cane, and fetish dress – too gross for me. I think

Vladimir went there – he's quite illiterate, but backed by family cash. You've seen how unrespectful he can be....'

'It all depends – what animals,' says Noura, backing off.

'Oh, the furries, not the scaly ones,' Ekaterina says.

'I'm fussy about who gets on my bed,' says Noura, sharpening scissors on a stone.

Ekaterina's a heavy type, proud of eye and stiff of neck. Noura thinks of opera, the swan who sails the boat. 'I'm scared of swans,' she says. 'Not fur nor scales – those birds are in between. They mate but once, monogamous, they leave a song but not a mark ... once into a couple with one, you don't get out.'

'What's it to be, Noura?' Ekaterina asks, losing patience.

'You'll find, says Noura, 'that the erotic is better written down, than when endured. It's more complete and pondered, you can keep it on a shelf, take it on trips, sends you to sleep – the best of company: once learned – it's a transplant in your heart. My question is – do you prefer poetry or prose? And just the twin size, plus a friend or two? Or the fantasies of kings and queens, full retinue, a bodyguard? – it being a reactionary mode the nobles are required ... to stand, watch, and applaud....'

'Poetry,' Ekaterina says. 'If that's the way it has to be – maybe you're right, and that way you will make your mark – pornographer....'

'Litterateur,' says Noura, giving the quickly finished album to her mate.

'I can't read this!' Ekaterina shouts. 'It's swirls and fingerings, and diacriticals, a nudge, a smudge, a curlicue, a long tail twitching on the margins, thickets of uprights, and the name of God comes in as well....'

'Oh, of course there's exclamations,' Noura says, proudly. 'It's an inexhaustible text, ever-ready – scrolls and arabesques; it's music and a menu ... a genital hors d'oeuvre of fennels and fortune cookies – beyond words, into calligraphy – my! it makes me randy just to think of it – the reed pen a whistling breath, a squeak, a long caress, then the grind of inks and pigments – a spurtle: black, red, yellow, green – then add the gold and lapis, entwine the rose and iris, plump up the carnal carnations, peonies as nipples in full flower, bond them in bindweed in the cartouches, add frames with lovers' bows, a cautionary love-lies-bleeding, possibly....'

'Yes, yes,' Ekaterina says, mightily aroused. 'But I can't read a word. Neither of us knows the alphabet they use here, and neither knows the other's....'

'So it must be,' says Noura. 'We each are strange planets – rare oddities of every shape and sensibility, inhabiting the dessicated caves and lakes, the piles of dust and fossil trees of bodies heavenly, profane of planets long abandoned ... emerging like Venus or Great Bears at dawn: a yawn, embracing the new day – astride a globe, a roundel of gas and rock – that day may last a year, or spin a second, then come as dark as dark, for centuries....'

'Stop, stop,' says Ekaterina, writhing. 'Too much, too much.'

'Lotuses, palmettes,' says Noura, without mercy. 'Thulth and Naskh – on rice-paper you can consume, digest: straw paper? ... or whippy birchbark? Sheep's parchment – with a pubic tufty twist attached, and at the end, your insurance, all being fair in pain and gratification, pleasure and excess – "in paradise a friend and security from the fire". No one wants to burn up in an experiment with crank-case oils, the alchemy of mixing ghee and ambergris, producing ... nothing. Absolutely nothing, nothing at all.'

'Quite unique, Noura,' Ekaterina gasps. 'This orgiastic wallow. No one would expect – with your disfavoured beetly face and mien – such depth....'

'It's unrepeatable, I fear,' Noura says. 'Take the manuscript, and pay me for it, pay me off. You can't be my boss now we have crossed, crisscrossed, so many intimacies....'

Somewhere, the book is *harum*: elsewhere, much prized and shown. The dedication shows Ekaterina is the star, her body mercury, untouchable, splayed out like the Kalahari.

The book is famous, Noura – quite unknown.

*

This is predation, Noura thinks: I'm stock, someone is narrating me, I'm a new empty vessel, rough stuff from Raqqa, a homely bowl demotic – jogging through my Bildungsroman. It's not me, I've been stolen, auctioned as street art. I'm emptied out. My book, though – a sensation; with sensation overstuffed.

*

'One last favour,' Noura says. 'Make me a beauty, Ekaterina. Or, if that's passé – my overhanging brow, the egg-plant lips, the Arcimboldo nose – that plantain! Clean me up, and make my eyes turn blue as space – make me a blank, no marks distinguishing, and no distinguished past that puts me on a list.'

That, Ekaterina does.

All Noura keeps – is Noura. Just the name.

'You can't do that,' Ekaterina says, too late. 'You must be what you are. Me and Vladimir – we shall always be bad drifting Russians. With Mongol ancestors, some Yakut. It's good, it makes me good, though Vladimir is not. I am at home inside myself....'

'I know I can't do what I've done,' says Noura. 'It's not to get an easy ride – I am myself inside.'

'Remember Byzantium,' Ekaterina says. 'The iconoclasts quite often won. Don't show your face, nor yet the face of God. Changing it – is even worse!'

They leave it there. If they've been bad – this is a good place to start, to seek salvation.

'Noura slipped away,' Ekaterina tells Vladimir. 'Changed aspect, unrecognisable. Her character was unknown before, and now, in a minority, what will she seem? Harridan or guru, bits of both? She's with the sky-eyes....

'You must stay as you are, but no one does. Suppose we all do what she did? You could write poetry, not prose – the heroes and the heroines slide off, transform – and yet, and yet ... inside, they don't.'

They laugh, they leaf through Noura's sexy text; even, maybe, they kiss. It's sentimental! Russians are.

Skimming an exciting book – it might excite. Trasgression's in the writing – it takes a special touch.... Mostly dullards read, in reading you do not transgress.

'Noura, with her new look, could run a charity for those she left back there,' says Vladimir. 'Everyone outside would trust her now. She could change the history ... war, revolution, if it occurs to her....'

'I didn't poke inside her head,' Ekaterina says. 'There's continuity there. I told her, don't think it's a rebirth: it's the death of what you were. She said, "It's good to see life from the other shore." An idiot!'

'Lots of people live like the stag, hunted into the stand of trees. It's a country here, and there's a fair amount of stags, though they're not eaten. The dogs and horses circle round, the horns sound their tunes. It's pastoral, you'd say,' says Vladimir, 'Your country's full of nature, then the dogs and huntsman go in, and they get you, and you're done.'

'There's a way out,' Ekaterina says. 'A little path I know, you trip on down it and change utterly, your antlers and your brown coat, your twitchy tail, drop off – and you walk out.'

'You'll need a document,' Vladimir says. 'And something more.'

*

Noura's face change – hasn't worked well. The nose heaves, cheeks droop. The eyes – two stagnant narcissus pools. 'I'll have to wear a niqab,' Noura thinks. 'What a bore!'

Tigrane, though, is fascinated by her. She has cosmological eyes, he thinks. He's yet to taste her grande cuisine, her sexy turn – he sees her as philosopher, a connoisseur of lived experience, useful for his plan ... those eyes, vacant as the skies, the rest concealed like the plots of sweet Sheherazade.

There's lots of sex in mysticism, he thinks ... sat there thinking, who's thoughts don't drift? Remember those old naked Indians at table, dribbling vindaloo.... He hasn't thought beyond that, besides, you can programme mysticism, not script it.

Tigrane – a button of a man, rich and alone. 'What do you want of me?' Noura asks, pushing him aside. He loves that. Insouciance – means idealism. 'A foundation in the Caucasus!' he says. 'A kind of *ashram*, bringing peace to those unruly guys, believers in all or nothing; in everything, smelted in the furnace and indestructable, women and men as fierce as lynxes or mosquitoes – all enemies, all perched on piles of history like faggots on a pyre. Burn, burn ... and up it goes. I'll bring enlightenment, a cool cool head, that talks of solid things .... It's my heritage. I shall leave it as I want....'

He thinks, he speaks – there's no filter.

And on he talks, of mud and sulphorous waters, leotards and contracts, spas and volley courts, parking for Buicks and for donkey carts.

'How much cash can you put in?' asks Noura. That's the test, of how long the folly lasts, she thinks. When it runs out, I'll be on the <u>road</u> again – meanwhile.... Love, death, belief, attachment -

'All so important,' Noura says. 'I've been in war zones. If only we had studied more....'

'Hmmm,' says Tigrane. 'I think – study yourself. All these subjects, books and such. They haven't changed a thing and – they're not compulsory. Study yourself, and do gymnastics.... Swedish drill. The Chinese warm-up, propeller in the stomach – Canadian steps, the Inca programme. Bodily discipline: eat what you want.'

'It sounds self-parody,' says Noura, 'but keep trying and the right combination will come up...'

'Different people live together, side by side, and in the next street,' Tigrane says '... yet, some places. like this one, and they can't. Countries – the same. Put oceans between them, still they'll fight....'

'I need to work on my course notes,' Noura says. 'I must admit – peace has never meant a lot to me.'

'Exactly,' Tigrane says. 'Study yourself. That's where it starts.'

What's new about the scheme, is you are paid for doing it: the more courses, training, that you do, the more cash you're given. It seems a recipe that can be extended – for everything and everyone. Now, you have mercenaries: and paid disciples preaching door-to-door – but this is revolutionary.

'Where'd you find your money, Tigrane?' Noura asks.

'In trees,' he says. 'And sand. And holes. And sailing on the sea and flying in the air. It's inexhaustible, until we've used up all the earth, turned it all to cash – and then.... We'll fly to somewhere else, and start again.'

They smile, they laugh. 'You see,' he says. 'What's simple – is easy too. I'm a creative. I do gymnastics, and eat what I like.'

That's chizhi pizhi – do not confuse with chichi.... 'Sounds like porn,' says Noura, and they laugh some more. Tigrane never learns of what Noura calls her smutty 'chap-book'.

'Kuchmachi too,' he says, a bit ashamed. 'The chickens! Terribly sad.'

'What's in this for you, Tigrane?' Noura asks.

'History,' he says. 'Vision. Tackling a problem. Besides, they put rich guys in jail to steal their cash, incarcerate poor guys to see them suffer. I want to be an in-between – rich, but not so much as yesterday.'

'In-between,' says Noura. 'Not rattlesnake nor wolf. A swan, in fact.'

Many people want to learn about the peace, and profit from it – so many they must decide: to let the peaceful ones in first – while brawlers make a fuss outside. Or let the tough nuts in, and have them fight inside.

Maybe here is the kernel of the end. The students are either hooligans or powder-puffs. Too bad.

The students love Noura, her eyes, the steadfastness, the faith – the urging them to seek a solitude, be stoic, even be ill-informed, not listen to their mates and family – reject their poisoned legacies. Be dirty, if they are: act it out, in feathers and mascara. Study themselves, in short.

*

There is a craze – to grow the tallest shrub – a cactus, wavering twenty metres up, grass high as a tower – or aloes broad, and manioc deep.... Everybody marvels – it's an achievement. With all-round peace, who knows how high they'd grow!

Tigrane's cash is pouring out. 'I'm nearly ready for the song,' he says. 'I'm out of tunes. Each song, like each swan, is different.... I'll work on it....'

'Tigrane!' says Noura. 'All swans are the same. There's but one swan, there's but one song. Everybody knows – those songs don't prove a thing. We're all the same, you say, like swans: except – we have no song. It makes no difference. At the last, we gargle and we croak – it functions for us, like it does for them – except it's just a rustle of our phlegm.'

The Tigrane interlude, his Academy, the list of faculty, publications, honorary doctorates, diplomas handed out, the balance sheet .... all ends in the archive, while the healing mud dries hard, the hydro-baths rust through, wistaria roots break up the tennis courts ... Only grasses stand heroic; a nymph or two might linger in the osiers.... The birds cluster by their size and colour, dispute, argue, fight.

Watch, learn!

'Don't take a lesson from them,' Noura says. 'That's just a fallacy.'

Tigrane takes offence. 'These hot summers and mild winters,' he says, 'Are they a fallacy? If I tell you there's a slight chance you could go to jail, Noura, and how sorry I would be – is that a fallacy as well?'

'You must have put me down for something,' Noura says. 'Abused me, my name. I told no one anything, no promises. "Think of themselves, stay out of trouble." It went down well. And you always paid me cash.'

'I had to puff you up,' Tigrane says. 'Everybody does it. Only a stickler thinks it's fraud. Anyway, a jail in Bielorus is better than top security in the States, if you should have the choice: there's theatre there, and time outside. Outside is relative – it means you're not enclosed so much.'

'Our bargain wasn't this,' she says.

'Here, it's beautiful,' he says. 'That was my point. It's paradise. The people – are the best, the most inventive and involved. They don't get on, is all. The history of the world is here, that no one cares about it, not history, and not the world....'

'You set me up,' she shouts. 'You'll be hung high – your neck will be a swan's, or longer still....'

That's the end. No more Tigrane.

And yet, she thinks, the times were good: walnuts and pomegranates, every kind of cheese. Before philosophy ... life as a sage.... What had she been? Her life before Tigrane – a blank, a nothingness. A scamper: no one, going nowhere.

*

Watching the black sea.

*

'I'm like the moon, Latif,' Noura says. 'My soul has a dark side.'

'The moon's all dark,' says Latif. 'The light comes from the sun, like for everyone. Besides, I have fine eyes – I see the dark, it's a veil that splits apart....'

Latif's a scruff. A sailor, not at home on land. He doesn't know Noura might be caught and jailed.

She doesn't know if she has personality – for sure, he's not concerned. Is it personality that attracts? – like honey draws on ants ... or is it cash? Or family?

'Forget my name,' he says. 'I've never been there. Don't speak the language, whichever one it is.'

'That's the state I'd like to reach,' says Noura. 'But beware! I'm not a safe port now.'

'Oh,' Latif says, 'It's the loneliness. Not that I have anything to say – but having no one, not a wall to write it on. 'I love you'! Or anything at all.'

'You'll be lonelier with me than with a wall,' she says.

'It's good,' he says. 'You don't cling. And I'm almost never here, or anywhere.'

'Being a couple helps,' she says. 'You probably have documents, or an excuse. A couple excites pity, understanding.

Singles can cut your throat and take your purse ... and if they don't, what else can they do for you?'

'That's my philosophy,' he says. 'A nutshell. A walnut, its two hemispheres. And there's always one who's left, to bury you.'

'I have a simple life right now,' says Noura. 'Does that make me simple? I don't know. I don't do agriculture, if that means simplicity....'

'My life is hauling other people's stuff,' Latif says. 'Not having any for myself. There's nowhere left to explore, and you can't get off – you must watch out, though, so's not to hit other things....'

'We've lots in common, Latif,' Noura says. 'Like millions of other people, many quite well off.'

They laugh.

'Imagination,' Noura says, 'is most of everything for me – fantasies of sex and conversation: tall trees: old stuff I find heaped up in my head....'

'It sounds precious,' Latif says. 'Aerated. We salts, we matelots – we leave imagination on the shore, or we wouldn't make it to another landfall.... You should experience being hunted, Noura, set up and jailed, importuned by your boss ... your dreads all concretised.'

'I know, I know:' says Noura, laughing. 'It all ends in imagination, just the same. I know – it's not a satisfying answer; and it hasn't made me happy. Quite the contrary: as if I lived on mud floors and crabapples to eat. I didn't live so's to be happy....'

*

I could do better than being with Latif, Noura thinks – but mostly
he won't be here.

She has odd ideas, Latif thinks: but mostly, I'll not be here.

They leave it there.

*

Then Latif thinks how Noura's been selected by a rich guy,
Tigrane – a solitary, a crook and dreamer, now gone to ground,
but still ... he had the eye. 'I can't stand being closed up in a ship,'
he tells Noura, 'Like in a row of prison cells, not seeing where
you're going to go. A metaphor, that's sure; but I could pilot you,
us both – to a success richly deserved, at last realised....'

'Make a plan then, Latif,' she says, 'if you're capable. For me,
it's all a test – not one you pass, but a profile will emerge. All
that happens to me, is my inventions. It's real, of course, and out
of my control, but it's an emanation of myself. I always win. You
think you can exploit me – I'm exploitable, and I'll let you go as
far as you like or dare – because it intrigues me. Are you such a
fool? Don't you know I see through you? What you do, you do
because of me – I'm always right, I always win. Always mine –
the top spot, even when you think you're fooling me. I recognise
your side – all sides. I'm smart, smarter than the clumsy world. I
win the being right, seeing through you. You all. That's my
success, my substance.'

'Excellent,' he says. 'I don't win like you, but I'm exactly as
I want. You're my resource, my wine butt in the corner. I can't
do without you, you're mine, I love you.'

'You're not a treasure, Latif,' Noura says. 'You don't try. You don't know how, you're thin as skin. I'm the tree, and you're my monkey.'

'It makes no sense,' Latif says. 'It's for both of us, my plan.'

'If I dreamt you, Latif,' Noura says, 'You'd be a scoundrel, and I'd have you caress me, and we'd laugh, I'd feel tender to you, and be sorry to have lost you when I woke. None of that's the case. Your desperation makes you clever, but the game's too big for you – you don't know the rules, don't have the stake. But still – how far will you go? Where will I end up? I always start over. I'm always more profound. You're always the same size ... and pasteboard....

'If I go to jail, I'll still have outplayed Tigrane. 'Study yourself?' – he can't, he's gossamer. 'Keep out of trouble?' – always good advice. Someone cheated in my case – but if I go to jail, I'll make the prisons furnaces....'

No one goes to prison for boasting, for vainglory. It would be interesting if they did. Money, sex or stupidity – that's what gets you into jail ... unless it's the wrong group you're in, the wrong enthusiasm, or standing too close to – the wrong enthusiasm, or the fear.

'If you have one man,' says Noura, 'you're sure to attract another one. It's like rhinoceros – the one without a girlfriend's curious, looking for a fight. Usually he's younger, slimmer, so he gets punched out. It's not serious for the woman, but you never know. Her suitor has potential, ambition....'

She's a bright bird with a cross beak. She sings and plays, and schemes, her brain fits in a foxglove bell, inside there's a psyche intricate as the caves of Dunhuang, and when she dies she's a wisp of flag on two fire-blackened twigs, a tissue: yes, she thinks, that's me. I'm wonderful.

Latif believes in me. What is he? Just a rower in the galley. What does he think my strength might be?

'I don't want to deal with capitalism,' Noura says, 'Not in any form. It's too easy to steal from it, and embarrassing when you're caught. Bureaucracies and parties? – you must lie, lie at the start; and then, upon that lie – about your usefulness, your sensitivity, your knowledge – build a castle where ghosts decide everything. Once in a while, you are alive to deny; for the rest – there's ghosts. I don't like that. Besides, you talk of change, but change comes unexpected, tiles falling on your head in a high wind.

'There's people who read a book, carefully, with memories turned on. I can't do that. I skim, I write another book over the one I'm reading, so neither's legible.

'I could act on stage. I could be a royal mistress, but kings and queens are dull as shitsticks. Or sing, be a virtuoso – but you're a slave to music written down, imagined sound...

'I could be a scientist – who invents religion, and proves the existence of a world of potent alien things that lives behind the wall. I could dream, I could confess, have everybody believe everything I want.... Or I don't want. I could make everybody be the genders and the colours that they like, the nationalities ... the believers and the sceptics of anything at all. Except – it's trivial! It's only interesting if you can't do all of this!'

Latif is shocked – Noura rejects what he hadn't even thought of.

'Or,' she says, 'I could just give up. You'd go back to sea. It means I've not understood a thing.'

'I don't want that, Noura,' says Latif, shaking. 'You haven't understood anything – not anything you could confirm. I'm pushing you towards results, achievements you can touch and frame.'

*

'I'm from a department of justice,' says Duff, easing off tall Mexican boots.

'I don't have strong feelings about justice,' Noura says. 'You do things indirect, justice comes indirect as well.'

'Oh well,' says Duff, 'justice differs according to where you are, and when you were, and what you thought you did. Recruiting, voyeurism, incitement, not reporting crimes, defamation, plagiarism. Anything that comes into your head: exposure and abuse....'

'I think we've all done those,' says Noura. 'I wanted peace – especially for myself.'

'Service of a foreign power. Spying, and unintended consequences.... Blasphemy comes in, and false pretences,' Duff proposes. 'You paid the clients to hear your philosophy. Where'd the cash come from?'

'I gave,' she says. 'Guidance I gave. They took. Maybe Tigrane took.... And gave – abundantly.'

Duff laughs, 'Oh,' he says. 'I was in Iraq. There was cash in boatloads given. Then I was all over; and I found all over everywhere there's cash – to buy the tents, to buy the arms, to buy informers and to build the jails.'

'I know all that,' says Noura. 'If I broke laws, I didn't see them written down....'

'You're supposed to know,' says Duff, squeezing her hand and screwing up his eyes in understanding. 'Natural justice. It should come to you unsummoned....'

'If I go to jail,' says Noura, much alarmed, 'If justice is natural, it could be anywhere.'

'It may be you're complicit; we all are,' Duff says. 'Neglect, avoidance. Leaving every scene. Misleading the young, disappointing the old.'

'Who sends you here?' asks Noura. 'What's done is done.... There's no complaints....'

'Tell me your plan,' says Duff.

'Latif must know,' says Noura. 'If there is. Perhaps you'll think a plan's a plot....'

'The past? Necessity? Are those your alibis?' Duff asks, taking a yellow legal pad from his leatherette case. 'The unintended consequences of ignorance or innocence, of gullibility, of superficiality, of dislike of your species and its claims, pretensions, its history, its promise of repentance ... your hint at "setting it all to rights", expunging sin and crime, hanging high the criminals and backsliders, the unbelievers, heretics, the rich and poor, the arrogant, submissives.... Taking and not taking people at their word....' Duff moistens his pencil with his tongue – it leaves a purple splash.

'Who seeks justice: who gains?' Noura asks. 'What does justice do for anyone? Console? A phase of mourning and recovery. I understand how people profit from injustice, but – from justice? Is there a link between them, what's the relationship, if there's one? I should have rewards, the just ones – but instead, the risk of punishment is always there....'

'Your followers, Noura,' Duff says. 'Suppose they start to kill. Is that your fault? Even a little? Self-absorption, "study yourself": the martyr, the assassin, the messiah, the psychotic – they "study themselves". "Don't get into trouble" – it means avoiding the consequences of what you do. Suppose there's injustice done to them; perceived, at least. What justifies a protest? Resistance? You don't specify, you leave it open. What does it mean? How do people react to what you say, if they are blocked? A guerrilla? Bombs? A revolution, civil war?'

'I can't be held responsible for what I've done and haven't done,' she says. 'I talk – people think, out of my knowledge and control. That's all – they are perverse and make mistakes. If you were interested, I'd tell you what I mean – but it's hypothetical. What I say and mean – that's just one plane. What I *do* is something else instead.

'It's a geology – how the real is layered and articulated. Press one stratum – others bend and fold. What's the relation between the state and market, myth and reality? Structure? Function? Dialectics or autonomy? How do I know how one project springs from, falls back on, all the rest.'

'Oh,' says Duff, 'we did all that at school. The answer is "who knows?" We need to find out what you thought, Noura ... but without inviting you to tell a tale....'

'Where'll you send her?' Latif asks.

'Listen,' says Duff. 'I'm one of you. I've known persecution. I'm here to help you, let you down softly.'

'So that no one hears?' Latif asks, not following.

Duff goes outside. He speaks to someone far away, it's incomprehensible.

'I'm a bit of a jacobin, Noura,' he says, returning. 'Forced to be free: that's what people must expect. Do you agree? It was a shibboleth....'

'No one ever asked me,' Noura says, 'to be free or not. I ride the storms. It sounds like terrorism, put like that.'

'Well,' says Duff, beaming, 'do you know any terrorists, Noura?'

'We'd not have wanted to discuss that,' she says. 'People from all over came. Will come.'

'See, Noura?' Latif says, angrily. 'You've meddled in their interests.'

*

Duff writes, *'She spends her life wondering what she's for. She's obviously done terrible things, or had them done to her. Time flows like water, she and her sea are indistinguishable. How long would it take to find the present in her, and discover her destination?'*

*

'They have a time,' Noura tells Latif, 'To hold you. There's a cost.'

'They have money, Noura, everyone knows that,' says Latif.

*

Duff leaves it there, puts Noura on a list, so whatever she decides to do, it's difficult. She's misunderstood. Everything is unpredictable, like it was before, but being on the list means some of the unpredicted people who peer into what she does – they write about her, a few lines. She's held responsible for things unknown to anyone.

'It makes no difference, Latif,' she says. 'We'll just go on until we hit the wall.'

'Duff was an idiot,' says Latif. 'Does it mean his masters are idiots too?'

'I expect they're a higher type of idiot,' Noura says. 'Wanting what we cannot give. Duff's terrified me, which is his strange job. We'll never be rid of any of them.'

'I wish we had more Chinese dropping in,' says Latif. 'They're fun. I'd love a laugh.'

'I haven't found it so,' says Noura. 'No one tells a story nowadays. But one keeps an open mind. Maybe we're vulnerable to foreigners, dropping in and threatening – especially as we're foreigners ourselves.'

'That takes some thinking over,' Latif says.

It's good there's a length of silence. Then Latif takes out a flattish disc of lead. 'This is a mystery,' he says. 'You could set up as expert, tell people what they've got – not illness! We know how that will end – I mean, things to understand.'

'It's a coin,' says Noura. 'Worn and worthless. You can see the river, the tiger, and the fish. That was a fine city once.'

Latif peers at it. 'There's nothing there, Noura,' he says. 'It's not a coin, it's always been quite blank. It's nacre, off a commode, I'll bet.'

Noura shrugs: you can't spend the disc, the city's gone. If you're an expert, you need another expert to disagree with. 'On your own, Latif,' she says, 'Knowing isn't fun. It's like life before the Chinese come.'

'Duff came,' he says, 'Because we live in this rook's nest – in the old town, all services are intermittent, and no one decent would live so cramped. No one drops in if you've big rooms. We have to find something to do that looks quite innocent.'

'We can't,' she says. 'We can't do manual work, and all brain work is suspect. Anywhere Tigrane left cash, or just his name – involves me. I could answer for him there, his money's run....'

'Like bilge,' says Latif. 'I could be a painter, except – I only do two colours.'

'I know,' says Noura, 'And you put paint on everything ... finish one room, and you start painting it again. Latif – you'll never paint on shore. You're mythic – Sisyphus.'

'We need a group,' Latif says, 'Young, innocents. We're taken seriously because we're past our prime. We've lived – it seems we take life seriously, think of a future when we've disappeared. We are a threat, like gardeners who plant landmines underneath the honeysuckle....'

*

'I suffer for all those I can't do justice to,' she says. 'I know what justice is – it's what they plead for, from me, from anyone, politicos and all. I drag myself, like a steel ball on my own leg, my past and present, snagged between what I might do and what I'm doing.'

'I've done a deal,' says Latif. 'I can do half a shift at night – baklava and bignés. The misshapen ones I can bring back – a feastfor us....'

'It's the other stuff they want you for,' she says. 'Carrying dodgy packages, at that hour – not patisseries for sure.'

He doesn't say, she doesn't press. A little dirty traffic on the side – it's an insurance, puts you in another class, doesn't need an explanation, no dictionary. A quite different squad of cops.

'I'm stepping back,' she says. 'I'm not shaping people any more. Fortune-telling. No cards, no guessing, no superficiality. This city's full of tall poppies who believe in magic. In the world – they all do, the powerful ones, the influential – they have magi who cast their day, astrologers, makers of talismans, cunjurors and tricksters.

'I'll do it properly – psychology and sociology. They'll sit here for hours, and I shall analyse them – how far can they go, how far will they? What will bring them down. I'll do a proper job, read them up, context and biography – and prophesy. They'll be dependent on me.... No, not what I want, but for a while – it works.'

'A muse to trash,' Latif says, impressed and disappointed.

'Who gives out justice, Latif?' she asks. 'Do you want some?'

Clearly, he doesn't. It's the thing he most dreads.

'There's many in the building,' he says. 'They were all forced to come. They'd all like justice – but you're into telling fortunes. Quite different. Quite the opposite.'

*

'What's that?' Noura asks. 'An eye – sees one way, the other sees the opposite?'

'It's a parrot,' says Latif. 'Sailors attract them. They all want to get away from where they are – then they regret, make that hoarse cry. Sorrow, revelation.'

'It could be my soul,' says Noura, offering her hand to be bitten.

'Yes, it could be,' says Latif, 'But it's still mortal. That's the catch.'

'Will it speak to me, or must I confide in it?' she asks.

'No,' he says. 'It mustn't talk – if it did, and comprehended, it wouldn't be an animal, but something in between,' he says.

'We're animals,' says Noura, puzzled. 'Like them. We speak and are not comprehended. There's no one outside to set a rule, it's all convention, worked out by ourselves ... the dialect, the gesture, the *smorfia* – the ideas that you tell and aren't believed or understood.'

Latif ceases to follow: it's a parrot. Fun. More fun than the absent Chinese. It's a small one, cover it, like it's not there.

'I have some generals and senators, Latif,' she says. 'Nowhere to put them when they wait.'

'Aha!' he says. 'Have them come with me, to eat baklava.'

And that they do – all have a sweet tooth, maybe more than one.

Noura foretells. For generals, it's easy: but how many colonels will make it to the top? That's tougher – then there's priests and candidates. Everybody wants to know – the future. If you know it – is it good? It may become a territory in-between – not present, not past – but not an unpredictable. A spectral scene.

Most people go on being as they are – those who face, who want, failure – maybe they are sharper ... maybe more cast down, maybe more fired up. Noura can change them all. Perhaps she warns of failure when she can't predict.... Do those want more justice? Or plan vendetta, a *faida*, drop out, conspire, slack off, repress and bully, kill themselves, their children and their lovers too – 'I ought to tell them first,' she thinks, 'how to handle what they'll be. It starts as curiosity, then becomes a hell or paradise when it's just a purgatory, like before.'

'Watch yourself,' says Latif, who's much prized in the cake emporium – 'They'll take revenge on you, whether they or you are right or wrong....'

'Maybe I could blame my success and failure on the parrot,' Noura says – 'Like the fraudsters blame it on the cards.'

I'm consistent, she thinks. If you study yourself, you'll know your future. And these guys make the trouble, they court it, don't avoid it.

'Latif,' she says, 'don't sign contracts. Don't buy longterm milk. There's a blockage coming! These colonels – they're redundant. So too – middle rankers everywhere. Priests, cops, politicos – no promotions – just frustration! Hard times, my dear. Get ready packed – the parrot's on alert. We must prepare to move, and run!'

'Calm, Noura,' Latif says. 'The answer is – sex shows. These guys are all obsessed with their careers and pay. Take their minds on to a hotter place....'

'I might arrange,' she says. 'If cakes do not suffice....'

And that she does. It doesn't change too much. She's seen her future, but she doesn't tell Latif he's nowhere in it, though the parrot is.

*

I'm an anomaly, she thinks: those who lose their faith along the way, who betray their class and country, their family, and all the people you mistake for friends and partners – you end up on your own and incommunicable. Anomalous – and waterless.... Up to the lookout of this tall thin building – the water cannot rise.

Our room, storm-tossed and gyring – any moment, we could be thrown down....

Here's a client: Gabi, marshal of police.

'Gabi!' says Noura. 'I love the smell of you! It surely cannot be the parrot – they're messy eaters, but spend time grooming and climbing where the wind runs free. But you – a marshal, even a Marschellin ... the fragrance! Knights of the thornless rose, and you, lady knights, what can I call them...?'

'Oh,' Gabi laughs, 'I don't go for little boys. If you prefer, I'll take off my boots and belt. And uniform, if you insist....'

And so she does, and stretches out beside Noura. 'It's oranges and jasmine, isn't it?' she asks. 'I ran the dog squad, and our noses were refined.... Your scent! Your underwear – mine's mostly gifts – commercial and snazzy – yours is crocheted, I'll swear....'

'No, actually, it's tatted. There's a sweet old crone who lives just two floors down – an introduction, if you want...?' Noura says, enchanted, swept along, her first cop friend expansive, longing for an intimate rapport, for sure....

So, they exchange some info and more compliments – it all goes smoothly, and Gabi concludes –

'I'm here this once – just to confirm my promotion's on its way....' and Noura says, 'My dear! Don't dwell on this – but I don't see you breathing, past this year. A shoot-out, or a bust-up – ending bad, real bad.... You should think of quick retirement – or at least, don't answer danger calls....'

'I can't do that,' says Gabi, starting to cry. 'I love the front line, peril, risk.... Where would I go? And the embarrassment....'

'You'd crouch down here,' says Noura. 'Wait, decide – enjoy the peace....' She's drunk with the proximity, the promise of a friendship, protection, the experience of managing extremes of uncertainty and power, but – in an instant she must face the cost of her predictions, unexpected rewards that slip away....

'Gabi, you're so direct!' she says, delighted, apprehensive.

'Oh Noura, everybody is these days. There isn't time to spar around and keep a distance,' Gabi says.

'I hadn't heard,' says Noura, taken aback. 'I'm alien to the customs here. And – is that a tiger on your back?'

'These ink tattos – I put a new one on each day,' says Gabi. 'Everyone in barracks does the same – or else we'd die of boredom and of fright.... They are our talismans....'

And she guides Noura's fingers over the shape. She shudders, passion or chill – Noura embraces her, and....

'Steady, Noura,' Gabi says, quite angry. 'That's not the road I'm showing you. Initiatives are mine; the news you bring me of my death – is devastating. I'm terrified. And is that patchouli you've got on? Suburban granny, Noura!' And she laughs.

'So,' she goes on, 'some louche toxic plans to shoot me down – I'm mortified! It could be your invention.... Some erotic prank....'

Obviously it is.

*

'We can't converse, Latif,' Noura says. 'We're trains on different tracks, bound for former capitals, now tourist spots.... But – I'm lost. Remember Duff – the idiot, who trapped me in that net of infinite length? The dark night, the blacklist? Now, Gabi turns up

– a new, direct sort of cop, who offers indifference and love. They seem the same: the cops too, I expect. What disillusion!

'You and I – we're parrots. Our problem is extinction, not fulfilment. Sailing! You don't sail, you haven't seen a sail for centuries, but still – that's what you say you do. And I – speaking philosophy? A joke. Fortunes? Another idiocy. A fortune in big cash – needs hiding, explanation, lies. And is denounced. I charge a fee – I don't bestow. Make your fortune for yourself.

'I sought a lover – instead, with Gabi I had an intimacy too close and sudden; quite ephemeral. A misunderstanding. The body – has come into dominance, Venus is eclipsed, then occluded by a strapping Hercules....

'The future – is a length of track that we must cover, knowing it won't bring us enjoyment. We're not become iron horses. And we've lost touch with evolution....'

Latif nods. It's hard to understand; or else – it's obvious. Times change, the two of them aren't changed with them. They're stuck in time and shape – like ageing parakeets. Duff was a hunter – Gabi – a tricky lover, or maybe high. Probably – she was high: cops relax with pills, and heat up with them when they've a risky job to do.

'There's nothing you can change, Noura,' he says. 'You think signals are still exchanged with flags. They aren't – now, it's all digital. Fingers, but no touching, and no fancy.'

*

'The idea was brilliant,' Noura says. 'The execution never bettered. But – it's lonely, telling fortunes. And the people who want to know their fate – what weird horrors, holders of power, dispensers of prejudice! They're the only ones who think the future's good, and that they'll be top cocks strutting in it.

'There's no proportion, no reflection. They stare in their mirror for so long the silvering wears off, and it becomes clear glass. They think they see the world clearly – really, it's their mirror that's worn out.'

'I have an idea,' Latif says. 'Let's get out of here. The window looks straight at, not through, another window opposite. We've no horizon but ourselves. Let's run a boat – take people to see dolphins. Live in a beach hut....'

On he talks.

'That's beautiful, Latif,' Noura says. 'The problem is – I can't stand you. I love the parrot, but you – are an ignoble trickster. I've seen you in the street – a little dog, a prick red and scaly, rearing on your crooked legs to set it into any hole. You're sour scum, Latif.'

'Opinions are free,' says Latif, apparently not put out. 'But you can't act as if your opinion freed you from me. You are responsible for me, and I for you.'

'I ask myself,' says Noura, not yielding, opening the window so it clashes with the window opposite just being opened ... 'What I'm responsible for, who to? Is it you, Latif? Or my state, that used to be a legal state and now is dissipated, suicided or assassinated, gone? Gone utterly. I'm not responsible for it, and it – is dead. No force, no contract, left. Some one, a clown, sits on the throne. Nothing to do with me. Where did the responsibility that once was claimed from me, obedience, legality, all that – where did it go? Should I have tried to save my state, fight for it, against its enemies? Did it think of me?'

'This is old stuff,' Latif says. 'If you leave, Noura, who pays the rent? And all those cops. You tell them you do nothing bad, that what you think, has no consequences.... Suppose it doesn't happen so?

'Study yourself? And find you're pure, and the world needs you to purify it, which takes a war, with victims – all war is civil war, uses the guillotine or butcher's knife.... Thinking leads anywhere, best not indulge, unless you're guilty, get banged up, wires thrust up your prick....'

'Oh, casuistry,' Noura says. 'I only ask – what does my responsibility mean, where does it start and stop, who decides my case ... does anyone have a responsibility for me, to save me, even from myself?'

'Yes. No. what difference does my answer make?' Latif asks. 'If you've no responsibility for me, you certainly have none for anyone; the guys in camps and jails.... You didn't put them there, you cannot get them out, besides – are you so sure what they deserve? Usually, the people compromise – "keep the camps and jails, but make them bearable". Is that responsibility?'

'I'm off, Latif,' says Noura, stuffing boas in plastic bags. 'Don't get into trouble. Study yourself. Reform!' She shouts the last word, slaloms down the narrow stairs, bouncing from bum to knee – 'Someone should fix this scree' she yells. She feels bad for Latif – maybe that's enough to make redress....

She skitters out into the street, sends the rubbish flying, holding her skinny battered arse, and Latif screams down after her, not about responsibility, that argument's been done and dead – throwing down some shelves and boxes, bits of stuff he can't replace, detergent, lavatory cleaner. It all does no good at all, some hits Noura, but most makes more mess in the street.

Everyone is on his side – a decent person wouldn't do what she has done, he's a poor man, no trade, stupid, no friends, lots of problems, bit of a thief, drunk or drugged mostly, but you understand, all in all, you don't want him in your house, but he's a good man, polite, hard grafting, sells stuff expensive but it doesn't go to him, and he makes those bignés, by night, excellent, good to the kids but not a molester, not a *pédé*. Not a meddler, nothing of a boss about him – unemployable in anything at all ... just lays out bignés on the trays.

Noura's let the parrot out ... it flutters, doesn't know what natural food is like, taps on the windows then flaps off when hands reach out; or bites – gets hit with brooms. 'Hey, hey!' Noura shouts up, contrite and pleading. Nothing, *nada* – the bird is terrified, has lost its poise, its culture, place. Flies off, quite slow, already tired: spreads out on a roof. Nothing. The end. Noura's responsible, so what? – it's done and finished, the beautiful creature, so courteous and delicate. Just too bad.

*

If Latif had wanted to plead, surely he'd have come to the bus station. He's not there, Anvar is. There's no escape – they are the only voyagers.

'Hey,' he says, 'You burnt the house down – did you leave survivors?'

'No,' Noura says. 'I'm a clinker.' It's true. Her hair is singed, as if she reads the Ramayana in bed.

Latif must have thrown the fire-pot down on her. 'Don't try anything with me,' she says. 'I had a practice as a witch – too many clients. I'm still sharp as a thorn.'

'The traffic here's to East and South,' he says. 'We're all poor busted flushes, taking our earnings back to our origins.'

'Not me,' says Noura. 'I keep climbing high and tumbling down – I take back the punishments I've earned – only for me. I've no one to share them with, or have them tell me why....'

'Oh,' Anvar says. 'It's easy. You're punished because you want to be. It shows what you have done has some significance. Recognise how it's been trivial – and you'll be free.'

'There's others,' Noura says.

'You're their punishment,' he says. 'They must make a case and stow you in it.'

'Is that all?' she asks. 'Life. Trivia and punishments?'

'There's luggage,' he says. 'But you have only accoutrements. You cannot settle. Choose a bus which shows a movie, comprehensible wherever it is bound. I saw The Magnificent Ambersons, in Kurdish. Don't let the language stand between you and the image.'

'Los Olvivados,' Noura says. 'The lost boys. Find me a bus that shows that.'

'Of course,' he says. 'You're right. There won't be one for years. This town – you could stay here, and save the fare. Did you leave someone somewhere who might be still alive?

'Forget. Remember. You'll see there's not much difference – not in how each gives different pleasures. You'll always be a soldier, despite all those defeats and desertions. Follow the clouds of dust. Horses, camels, feet and hooves. Find a corpse, take their insignia, a sword, a gun, a spoon: their paybook. Even those antique armies had a forestful of leaves – Justin says at Marathon – 'six hundred thousand Persians'! All those letters home! the photos! No one will find you there, you're all unknown soldiers – it's hard to be the chosen one of those, that gets the everlasting flame – though you all qualify.'

'I know my destiny,' says Noura, 'but....' Suppose I get on the wrong bus, she thinks: or miss it. Perhaps that's the way to lose my trail.

'I couldn't stand being beside you on a bus,' she tells Anvar. 'Sitting quiet while you rhyme the landscapes. Better stay here with you than that. This way I'd avoid the mountains....' the bus sliding down where the road collapses, then rolling over and over: a pine cone or a skittle. Losing shape. All dead.

Or ransomed when the local ceasefire with the guerillas has worn out. All lying under low muslin tents, the sun stares, the military drones, kestrels, overhead – you shut your eye in case a dart drops down, right on the target. Nothing to eat or drink.

'With most of your fame ahead,' says Anvar, 'you're oddly centred on impotence and convalescence.'

'Why did they fire you, Anvar?' Noura asks. 'Was it from something? You're bristling with command....'

'Oh, there were plots,' he says. 'You know them too. Women – young girls really. They love to make a conquest, boast about it. You suffer for it every way.'

'And you were foolish?' and she laughs. 'How banal! Caught fiddling while the adolescents burn! Anyway, you're right: I am headed for great things, and the great disillusion too: with all of you. I'm my masterpiece.'

'Oh, I've no doubt you're much much more,' Anvar says. 'I think, if we could read you, we should all be wise and chastened.'

'And I'm sure you won't be,' Noura says, quite reassured.

She doesn't ask how he regained authority. Now, he lives by sponsorship: friendship is the door to ownership. If he helps you,

you are his, his property. Don't forget. He runs everything that isn't serious, what's serious is that the ship of state won't sink. Noura is anything to him, and nothing for herself. Mistress, wife or prostitute: minister, showgirl, governess to someone's kids. He's a piece of luck for her.

*

'It's not just me,' says Anvar. 'I go right to the top. Know everybody on the way – the top, of course, is not the top of everything. The top – is of the middle, but there, I know them all.'

'What must I do?' Noura asks, excited, apprehensive. 'I have no choice, but, of course, I can fail, and disappoint you – be disobedient, unreliable. That's my escape....'

'Or it's you permanently,' says Anvar, quite severe. 'We'll have to launder you. All these cops around you! Once in, you can't leave, not by walking out, resigned. "Study yourself" – remember what Lenin said; "dream actively". Imagine, act, and what you dream becomes reality. That's what we have heard, and it's just what we don't want. Can we find a way to steer you round that rock, and lay you, Aphrodite, on the beach?'

'Well,' says Noura, 'Now, we're all a bit of communist, and maybe even more of capitalist.... It's restoration – waiting for another Empire, we're back to kings and queens.'

'"Keep out of trouble", like you say – translated it might mean "don't get caught",' he says.

'Yes,' says Noura, 'yes, it might.'

'You must be an optimist,' says Anvar. 'Cheer us up. Don't be a fugitive – don't suggest that what we have could countenance alternatives.'

'I'm not a person people like,' says Noura, 'and not a person who likes people.'

'That's fine,' says Anvar. 'You won't need ask questions – everything about our place and us is obvious. In the encyclopedia, in a few lines: all true. You won't stick out. If you did, we'd cover you. Whatever you have done, won't cause surprise.... We are a refuge. The bus station – that's where you find the eternal travellers. No one likes them. They're creative.'

It's a fraud, but after all ... that's nothing special.

'I'm sure there's lots to do,' she says. 'I'm loyal, but not enough for martyrdom, whatever your cause may be.'

'You don't need steal or scheme,' says Anvar, 'or pretend. Struggling countries – they all have dedicated people, interesting alcoves. Everywhere is struggling.'

'I'd always heard,' says Noura, 'if you're at the bus station, not knowing which bus to take – there's always a chance you'll be recruited. Sometimes you end naked and dead in a hole under the stairs, other times – as a counsellor. Someone must be found for both scenarios. As they say, a roll of the dice will never abolish chance.'

'I bet you've used that quote before,' says Anvar. 'Unfortunately, it's true and leaves nothing further to be said. Too bad it's not your own invention. Your predictions – they're well known, well researched. Not quite a fraud, not quite intended to be true. Well done!'

THE TEST

A country is a strange reality. Anvar's has been beautiful, they say, if you ignore the arid parts, the dried-out mountains, and the rest. The poverty – Anvar and his bosses, they don't help! Who does?

It's best to keep clear of the cash aspects. It's normal, regular – don't fret, don't fantasise. Culture – brings prestige and visitors – an *isola felice*. Artefacts and shows – talent and favouritism. Mostly you don't die of it.

She writes it all down. In the long room, there must be four hundred candidates. Most have the plastic bags they carried, all they had, while waiting for a bus. Some have long beards, some bare bellies, platform shoes. Some are fragrant, some just smell. The hall is lined with mirrors, so it seems your ghosts are waiting for the test along with you, when you look up, the ceiling's full of flesh, suspended in a fantasy – short pricks, neat nipples, shaven crotches, but an air of insistence ... not sex, not revelation ... A profane occasion, an exultation – but in the nude – all eyeing everyone, making a pyramid, eating fruit to keep that flesh pink-toned – a token black, hmmm – probably a slave, a body-servant, no orientals, all males lightly bearded ... and from somewhere there's a shout:

'You have an infinite time to make your bid. The selection will take place, however, in a day. No food, no sleep and no canoodling. You may cheat and copy what you like, bring in your electronic tools, write on your arms. We may select no one at all. There are no jobs, no rights, no terms – the conditions are delightful, times are indeterminate but probably – they're short.

No one can leave the hall before the owl flies or the bats go home. Deaths – will not be recorded.'

A paper's handed out – the usher, fully clothed, gives it to those he fancies, and the rest must beg or steal a copy. Each set of questions – or there may be one, or none – may be directed at the individual candidate.

Noura believes she's been selected for her style, her veil: her options are for security, or for folklore.

'How would you choose – between the need to find an epic for the nation.... And a map that justifies a war with our most tranquil neighbour...?'

'The epic *is* a map,' writes Noura, though the paper says, 'only a digital alphabet can be recognised. Write your answers on both sides of the paper – remember, you can only use a zero or a one. No human will be involved in your evaluation....'

... 'Four hundred thousand lines is way too long,' she thinks. 'Our epic will describe an expedition to the peaceful folks beyond the hills. The intention was to massacre. Evidently a sally unsuccessful, it had best be short – a limerick would do, an epigram....' That's it. Something like, 'We came, we saw, we lost....'

She has another day, less the five minutes spent, to go. There's soldiers on the doors. She sleeps.

Did Mallarmé write something quotable on expeditions? All art – political resistance...? France – all that empire, jacqueries, the clashes on the Nile, the Prussians – 'the impotent poet, cursing his genius across a sterile desert of aches....': it catches Rimbaud and the Touaregs, the nation's trudge through sand to insignificance ... to cultural nobility.... She wakes. Best not be too clever ... don't set down the clinching thoughts....

Anvar takes her arm, the paper – and they bustle through the sleeping competitors – out the door. The soldiers present arms.

'You've won,' says Anvar. 'It's genius. Don't compose the epic yet – we'll give a prize to kids for that.'

'And all the others?' Noura asks.

'All will get a prize,' he says. 'For some, the chance to enter other competitions. Others – a thick steak, or a falafel ... competition is a ritual of life – *speculum mentis*: it's apt. Those who deserve – will get the least, those who aspire and imitate – the steak, *al sangue*.

'Some are bad guys, picked up trying to escape. We'll sell those on – there's what's called a terrorist quota. If we collaborate, we get rewards. You, Noura – we shall liberate....'

She holds to her veil – he tugs, and off it comes. 'If I want it, I must do it by myself,' she says.

Too late!

Much here is a copy of somewhere that was never built, or not composed or painted.

What is original is very old and difficult.

Anvar says, 'In modern places, people like us start rich and end up very rich. I started poor, with luck, I'll end up rich.'

If you don't scheme, there's lots of time to fill. The spectacles, the festivals and shows and singing, dancing, boostering – all are done by people who believe in them. Noura learns to play the bagpipe. It's very very difficult – the instrument is out of whack – the pipes go from wide to narrow, the sound is nasal and the scale obscure. If you're a virtuoso, you must learn to sing as if you're another kind of bagpipe, a descanting evil twin, climbing up the stair into the blue – so high your voice has left your sex behind, a feather rising in a spiral, disappearing, never coming down. Even if you're talented, you might as well not start.

*

'You've not got far, toying with that doodlesack,' says Anvar, blowing into it, producing a coarse grave note.

'This work I do,' says Noura. 'Is attempted resurrection. People used to dance and sing, and make their rhymes, and tell their tales – it all had meaning and the meaning gave to them – another, deeper meaning.'

They were wrong, but still ... a lie that everyone believes is on the way to being true.

'It's better that it stops,' she says. 'Let it die. Culture, art – made at home, on spec, may interest, or not. It's of no substance – let it die in peace. Science is king, but gives us no meaning, except explaining how to use the tools to find out more; that we don't have meaning, not the sort that people wanted, anyway. So, let all that die – the dance, the song....

'Revive and copy, strut and strum: restore. But not with my encouragement.

'As for this polity – repression's against common sense, and everybody knows – we are all equal, even those bullying us.... That we are all equal was evident at the start, at birth. Each, in a general way, is indispensable to the whole. It means now we can all vote, or that we shall be oppressed.... Or both at once. What we can't do – is be in control, not of anything, anything at all, ourselves or anybody else....'

'I'm disappointed, naturally,' Anvar says. 'I always trust my judgement – first, I thought you gifted. Now I see – you have no

gift – you're sharp, you see through everything, yourself as well
.... You give nothing but the truth; transparent, intangible,
unloved, unwanted, ugly, with no friends.

In general, I was right, but I undervalued just how bright you
are. Too bad. There'll have to be a process putting you in reverse
... another competition, writing on the glass to show you're
wanting, mirror-writing as a spell undoing what we cast before
... the whole performance – back to front.'

'I'm sure there is another way,' Noura says, resigned,
resigning, with a sigh.

'There was Sufism,' Anvar says, brisk, dismissive. 'You have
the face and suety body for acting Shame or Trash. Queen of
statement – without subjects. Or there are undergrounds:
mysticism, research, terror, charity. But you turned your back on
all those. And failed in what you chose.'

'I don't seek humiliation,' Noura says. 'Let's keep it private.'

'There is the bus station,' Anvar says. 'No fuss, no fare.
Wherever. Wherever you decide, I'll write a note to say you left
because you were too competent, we couldn't stand your light
and heat ...The drivers know me – they won't ask, and you've no
luggage. Just the truth .... your speciality. I'll write....'

And that he does, and that she does – she takes the bus. Back.
Reverse.

*

I lost my soul, she thinks: it died. The parrot – flying to the
highest bough, then higher. Expired. I don't miss my soul, not at
all. I do miss the parrot. People expect to lose their soul, long

before they die; their minds dissolve; the *Geist* – like strawberry icecream, goes to nothing ... leaves a stain.

I must keep quiet – a place like this is full of spies, informers – who don't inform me, inform *on* me. Now, I've worked for a state – so, I know terrorists. They're like the pyramids, states. They make a shape, identical to other shapes across the plain, the desert – rearing to a point, the point being to guard the dead chief somewhere far down, the hideyhole, a secret chamber, looted over and over, but still the corpse remains, hidden apart, enjoying heaven. And the soldiers! All around, in the examination rooms, the movies, the *vernissages* – and the planes and rockets, the gas, the threats .... Study, I said, study yourself – don't worship yourself or anyone. Don't say what you believe, you'll suffer for it – besides, you don't believe – you guess, hypothesise. Don't know.

It's dawn.

'Are you afraid?' asks the guy, sitting down beside her, waiting, offering a piece of sausage, pink as a wattle.... 'Tell me what you fear.'

'Oh, it would take too long,' says Noura, and she laughs. 'It's what everybody fears, but I put it all together, it's my skin....'

'Remember the war?' he asks. 'You're sat where the bus leaves for where there were the massacres, the bombing – now, the suffering.'

'There's lots of stops like that,' she says. 'I've no opinion. You'll have nothing to report on, not from me.'

'Oh,' he says, 'Trust me. I'm on your side. Stick close to me, you'll get on for free. You'll have a reference from your boss, for sure ... show that.'

'Benign, malign,' she says, 'Whatever it may be, it *is*. I could worship that, perhaps. Worship what is – it won't take up much time. For what the guys down there went through ... what was, will take up thirty years more to suffer; each year remembering each year more thoroughly. And thirty more years, and then we're gone....

'State terror, terror without the state. Terror all round, millions of us. Terrorising, terrorised....'

She shivers, and he makes to put his arm around.

Here's the bus! Get on quick.

The guy thinks – 'Harmless: a wreck.'

Noura thinks how her life has been full of successes, but they might as well have been disasters.... Create some distance – after all, Anvar was a *guiren*, a person of importance who pushes you up the ladder. That's a metaphor – you don't hurt when you fall off. You're where you were. I'd make a good Chinese, she thinks – if only I could get over the anxiety they all have. Maybe as a party member? – but that wouldn't do me well here, the cops would wonder what I represent. And when I try to be obedient – people think I'm mocking them. Maybe they're right.

I've had wonderful accomplishments, escaped, kept my fearskin, been taken up and dropped, dropped the dregs myself ... now, I'm in motion. Those must be the Iron Gates, there's the sweet waters of Asia, and there's red peppers drying in the sun ... all these people, weeping for people dead or jailed – and I don't remember anyone, no one I value greatly, and it's mutual.

'All this next year will be under water,' says a guy.

'Water's good,' says Noura. 'We need it.'

'It isn't for itself,' he says. 'It's just a force to make another force – electricity.'

'Nothing's ever for itself,' she says. 'Like us. We're not loved for what we are, we're a force that may produce another force.'

The guy pulls away, he doesn't want proposals from Noura – she looks religious, mighty serious. A sententious bore.

All these guys, she thinks: all know about life, anxious to share it with you, none doing anything with what they know. When I get off, I must be different, be more, be less. Be something.

The guys you meet in transit – surely they should be talking rights, democracy? They don't do much themselves, so with others, protected – surely, they could act? They don't seem to think of that – perhaps we're all in movement, fluid, experimental, uncommitted – on the bus or waiting for it.

*

In the middle of the forest, a guy gets on, sits beside her.

'Enough culling for now,' he says. 'The fashion says it's time to plant small trees. They're like the turtles – one in a thousand will survive, if they all did – what a plague: an infestation.'

Not much to say to that – he's in the trade, and so must know, or have been told.

'We live in counter-rvolutionary times,' he says. 'No revolution, no Bonaparte, no Waterloo. Just destructions. No justice. Police and fixers – Fouché and Talleyrand.'

'I have no prejudice against destruction,' Noura says, feeling she must join in. 'If there is justice; but there never is.'

'Aha!' says the guy. 'You score a point. My name is Salah. I stand for doing what is right. That's justice? You say I don't exist. That means I'm crime. And you accept destruction – that makes you Vice. I die a miserable death – and you – a miserable restoration. The new? – A coarse America, with its bellyful of slaves...?'

They gaze out at the forest, flickering past. 'There used to be two types of tree,' says Salah. 'The bushy top, the pine. Now, there is one – the Mediterranean pine – a stem, a bushy top.'

It isn't true. Noura registers that Salah talks for effect, that contradicts what you can see. Napoleons – regiments of them ... Perhaps, she thinks, that is the characteristic of crime: while my contradictoriness must show that I am vice. Vice is a distortion – alas, not desire satisfied but appetite bulimic – stuffed and voided ... gobble and puke.

'How do you see us ending up?' asks Salah. 'The loggers' track that leads us to the shade, the dark: the cool – or the broad highway that speeds us on to where the bridge is – maybe – down?'

'I hadn't thought,' she says. That isn't so.

She sees a world all green, all trees, the mountains and the skyscrapers covered in foliage – no people.

*

She's the only one who gets off in the town. She wonders – is this where there was the war? Or just assassinations, poverty, or riches she's forgotten to accumulate? It's confusing, and Noura's at the age when confusion is the norm – two things to do at once, you're flustered, flounder, there's a stasis: blank.

People go silent when she's around – in the bar. The barman says they don't have Jack Daniels anyway – it seems to him she's asking after an acquaintance.

'You got off too soon,' says Salah. 'This here's the centre. The centre of the world, or once was – every inch fought over recently, you can't say it was a copy of what happens everywhere, even when there's only cows and maize to fight about – you can't say they re-invented concentration camps, or crusades, because no one had ever forgotten them or ever will.'

'I want to forget all that,' says Noura. 'This is my chance – here, or somewhere like, to leave my mark. A blot that covers, replaces, other blots.'

They're not our friends here, in the centre or the suburbs. We must be our ghosts. They ignore us, talk through us, don't hear us, shut the door on us.

It's like they read us, a wrong name, tagged with the wrong origin, wrong kind of disenchantment, wrong songs in our head – wrong subspecies, that might misbreed with them if they get too close to our wrong mouths.

The crows, *cornacchie:* they've an intelligence, a coarse wit, a devil-may-care, *insouciance* – it's all taken absolutely seriously, but with a dash, a swagger – and the eyes don't miss anything. They watch us too, although there's so much to be watched, they miss nothing, don't judge, aren't scared, don't interfere, don't care, and are not cared for ...we hardly see them, or listen to their arguments, but they're aware of everything around them, maybe they're short of an aesthetic sense, but here the people haven't had one of those for nearly three centuries, since when the money ran out, or it ran away to breed more rapidly.

'I see why people love this place, it's home wherever they have gone, not coming back, not ever, if they did – much worse than death, Salah,' she says.

'I've business here,' he says. 'You've nothing, Noura. It's your last place, I'm sure, but it doesn't mean you'll get anything from it. These are *Neinsagers*, experts at it, have always been, know nothing but refusal and rejection. Injustice came naturally ... it always will. I'll finish my life here, trying to do justice, with dossiers that tell lies.'

'A judge with no jurisdiction,' Noura says. 'Salah. Frustration. I'm glad I never took a fancy name.'

'You're clean, Noura,' Salah says. 'Tell them what you've learned. I accept – there is no justice. Try another tack....'

'I'll tell them,' Noura says, 'I'll give you happiness. Some, of course, resist, will never ever feel what is called happiness. To those, I'll give my wisdom.'

'Happy or wise,' says Salah, much impressed. 'I'll call a meeting. Everyone should come....'

He does; they do. There's flummery, and introductions, points of order, proposals for a compromise, but in the end – she gets to speak.

'I give a consolation,' Noura says, seeing the town, the city – country – mute, excited, listening. 'Happiness: or, at the worst, knowledge enhanced: what is called wisdom. And for free.'

'Speak, speak – yes! Yes!' they cry.

'We are a species,' Noura says, 'And we profess our common fate. Our death, our luck and destiny, being the topmost dog. We're versatile, we move around, we're universal. Persecute us – we find another place. Starve us and beat us – we'll resist, then run away. We're great survivors, endure slavery, justify our dominance, insult and lie to keep our perch, exterminate, train bands to make the victory parades.

'What I propose is change and change about. Each day – or maybe every two – we change our house, our work – or unemployment, if we wish or must – our family. We live with others, do another job, exchange our interests, our kids, our dogs and cats. That way we share our skills and principles – go to the church or temple, mosque, or stay away, pray, curse, cast spells or spread our compost on the fields .... drink vodka or strong *chai*, eat goat or fiddleheads, wear dishdashas or go nude, burn incense or the dead.... That way we'll see how strong is our belief in family, community, and action that's productive or at least – is meaningful. Part divine, part a submission.

'We'll test the concepts that express our moods and values, test the patience of our lookalikes to suffer our mistakes and arrogance, and so we shall become aware of all that makes us various and human. We shall be individual, but also interchangeable – we'll do each others' work, take their responsibilities – and then move on ... We'll be completed – animals of genius and versatility. If, by chance, it doesn't make us happy – then we'll have reached the limits of our understanding, of our abilities. We shall be wise....'

She remembers all that time with Latif, the dirty deals in the regime with Anvar. Permanence – 'that is a killer', Noura thinks. Staying in lousy relationships, crap jobs, being a slave or master, filthy rich or stinking poor. Change, not wandering – trudging round, that's trash, and trivial. No! Settlement, but endless change. That's evolution, adaptation, transforming our environment – it's what we're made for. What we say, that is. Only thus we'll demonstrate how we are tops – up on the food chain, eating everything that moves and's served in chafing dishes, desiring everything – riches untold and exploitation of the weak, enslavement and resistance, capitalism, socialism and a noble anarchy .... covetting the beautiful, the young, the sexy and the frigid, the hairy and the bald.... We shall be wholly human.... At last – we shall be Prometheus unchained, rampaging, all things to all women and all men.'

There's a buzz, some faint: most turn to neighbours never seen before and say 'it's mad!'

'This, my fellow humans,' Noura says, 'Is the first step to happiness. Persist, experiment. It also happens to be wise.'

No one likes Noura's attitude. Even less, what she suggests. A sage says, 'Maybe you've not understood – history brings us hatred from far back – these traitors in our midst – we've always hated and mistrusted them....'

'That's fine,' says Noura. 'I don't suggest banal acceptance of what comes from standing in another's shoe, knowing each others' size of feet. Bring your hatred to whatever place you go – it's precious and an indicator of attachment – I don't judge, and Salah here has no jurisdiction..... If we fail – so be it. It's too bad. We aren't what we set out to be – the good and bad conjoined, the ever-evolving, the bright stars.'

Later, she says to Salah, 'We started off just picking up our food and killing it: then, we were territorial, sticking to our land, our possessions – but we were inventive. We found out, we can buy and sell our land, and we've invented money, so we can put our soil into our pocket – just like Freud said, it's nightsoil, daysoil too – and we can carry it around, and bank it if we trust those guys ... and families: they're territory, possessions, but they have a money value too ... they are our herd of similars, but mix them on to other herds – and they grow mightily, they interbreed, they swap their brands, they're cows on speed, or sheep on acid

– marry, divorce, adopt, bequeath – we manage relatives like they were thoroughbreds, bred to run on flat or over hurdles ... they're all labour, all potential profit, in the act or in the bud.... And as you move on round – it will not change, no, not at all, it's an experiment, a test, but endless changing means you won't forever be a frightened rich guy, or resentful poor. Next day, you turn and turn about ... your fortunes are transformed, and then, and then....'

'I understand all that,' says Salah, 'but me and you, maybe we are the only ones who understand, and also think your idea is marvellous.... And yet – you don't join in....'

'It's evident I'm wise,' she says. 'I thought this up. For sure, I don't join in. If you're wise, you don't want happiness, unless you're stupid. And besides – the people here, they ostracised me. They need the happy cure more than the rest.'

There's cheating. The rich pay off the poor, the poor blackmail the rich and ransom them. That brings them happiness, and – they are just the stupid ones. Where it goes well – the rich enjoy the food of poverty, they grew up on it, and the poor – they overdo the food and drink, and so don't break too many sex taboos. In short – the stereotypes prevail, and some are mostly wise and happy with that too. The idea is – you keep the test continuing till the end's secured. Who knows how long it takes? Hares, weasels – they're quite happy, and quite wise. Maybe they had a Noura talk to them – and made a compromise: a life of instincts, passing fun – burrows and huntsmen, foxes and disease ... no clothes, no walking erect or with a stick: no cinema, no Stolichnaya vodka ... lives short and sometimes sweet.

'Justice' – knows no politics, they say. That's Salah – just a lawyer. Law in the service of power – usually called Crime, by idealists, at least.

So too, Noura's 'test' – ignores a left, a right. That way – it's pointless – and reactionary.... 'No, no,' says Noura. 'I admit no criticism, even if you're right.' And there – she lets it stand.

*

'That was a splendour,' Salah says, 'Although it melted into nothingness. Now, Noura, you'll be made to pay. All the mistakes, the losses, and the breakdowns. Prepare for the tribunals. All your fault; endless cases, and up to me to judge.'

'Oh,' Noura says. 'I deny it all. I made no mistakes and caused no problems. Anyway, I have no cash – I spent all I had on bus tickets. Investing in kilometers, I'll go round the world – a little slower than by flight, but more anonymous, and get off where I want.'

'Your seed,' says Salah, thinking he should console, 'Is planted. One day....'

'You don't know me, Salah, not at all,' says Noura, and she laughs. 'I don't care. I don't love the species, I've no bet on whether it is destined to fulfil its boasts and hopes, or whether it will last and last, expressing grand desires and never satisfying them. To me – it makes no difference at all. In this respect, I stand with science. Either humankind achieves the immortality it craves: reward or recognition for its goodness, a progress indefinite and smooth – or it does not.

'My intuition, as a gambling girl – is strong. A million years of mediocrity, a day of fire – I've no idea. Will it be that? But – miracles are rare!

'If the good people here, and the bad, decide to give their lives a whirl – good luck to them. Not many have, and those will cheat. Whether they're good or bad – it doesn't matter, not a bit. The scheme is everything – it's indifferent to the result.... Happiness, or wisdom – nothing more. No prizes for achievement, no prevision for next week.'

'Well, fuck that,' says Salah, much annoyed. 'I have to deal with stupid claims, false witness, and bald lies. You take the bus, and disappear.'

'Yes, in a way it's so, it seems that way,' says Noura. 'Except – I leave your sight. I do not disappear.'

'They'll remember you, Noura. You've been a revelation,' Salah says, to flatter, give himself importance. 'You missed the chance, though – popularity outside the law. Sabotaging – lignite mines and airports, dams and abattoirs. Instead – your notion is granitic – radical and fluid seemingly, but nonetheless, it's a rocky outcrop. Uncompromising, dark – or should I say: backlit.'

'They don't know my life,' she says, 'They don't know where my idea started from. Besides, whenever you have freed yourself from something, or from someone – you'll find you've made another set of chains, much stronger; no padlock and no key. I didn't deal with that – I have a ticket, after all: and I can leave.

'I've only lived in yesterdays, known withered people from eroded plains. There's new types, made of caustic and titanium, foul of mouth and body, with basalt brains ... Human robots who've copied the mechanicals.... My fault, I don't know how to talk to them, nor they to me.... The others – I don't believe we ever talked – no time, no wish, no substance.'

She keens; self-pity a cold flux. There's not much you can add to that.

*

Maybe it's best to walk – people might recognise me on a bus, thinks Noura. Veil? No veil.

It's tiring, wandering up and down; these suburbs – compounds, closed gates with strident dogs behind.

Here's a guy, sweeping the street, so soft – 'I don't clean,' he says, 'I move dirt from there to here.' He confides – 'We're locusts. We – darken the skies. It's useless – our junk will suffocate us all. Eat and excrete – is all we know. Our excrement will mount and peak like Popocatapetls, everywhere....'

'Like pyramids,' says Noura. 'No fire, no flame. Just monuments.'

'Despite it all,' the guys says, 'I am an optimist. With the knowledge we all have....'

'Yes, certainly,' says Noura. 'What use is pessimism? If not the knowledge, then there's wisdom. For certain, that will serve.'

*

She sets out with determination, with the firm step of one who has at last in view a definite destination.

THE SCARF

I HAD AN important motive, taking the train to the city. I didn't want to do what had to be done, so when the woman opposite touched my foot with hers, I played the game, went on – a brief encounter, this train notorious for wanderers, people going to sell stuff, or coming back with stuff unsold. Solitudes sticking together, like unmatched pieces of two broken pots.

The climax in the park, clothed and furtive, wasn't satisfactory. That evening, we went back to my room. I could not apologise for anything, not the room, or the time passed in it. If I had died that night, they could have thrown all my belongings in the pit with me. Nothing of interest.

'You've got books, even,' she said, 'People must have wasted money having you taught....'

We didn't feel like more sex. She was very young, her face greasy and coarse, not quite as I'd imagined all that day.

That's it. A mistake, except you can't call meeting people on your way, by chance, it seems – mistakes. The mistake is you.

She says, 'You owe me. How do you go settle it? You dishonoured me. Did you think you'd bought me?'

'We were equal, Vinciane,' I say. 'No familiarity, no fee.'

'Honour's not a thing that individuals can negotiate,' she says. 'It's a concept. Honour inheres, it comes with other values, all tied up with coloured ribbon. It's acknowledged – by all our referents; families, our history: people alive, unknown, and dead – a line of tombs stretching back and getting smaller as we did, until we're back on all fours, eating lychees, our butts waving, long feathery tails. Buried shallow, abandoned, naked in the red soil.'

I'm terrified. Honour's an unexplored continent, a remote Bermuda. Blackmail, ransom, forced marriage, bride price, beaten up, killed, decapitated, eviscerated, ruined, incacerated – the imagination's clothed with geographies of words ... a coroners' clutch of pathologies within.

'I don't have your faith, your community, if that's what you have,' I say.

'I have the same as you,' she says. 'And it's not about gender, or taking something and getting something back: it's about duty to other people.'

'That's invisible. There are no rules, no tariffs,' I say.

'Exactly. That's my point. Besides, I must have a duty to you,' she says.

'I don't want it,' I say. 'Besides, what passed between us – I don't value. You're no more than anyone.'

'Yes,' she says. 'That's it exactly.'

'Well,' I say, 'Is it honour or duty?'

'When I reflect,' she says, 'It's duty. Honour would be a subhead only.'

'Forget it,' I say, in hope. 'It was chance.'

'It's all chance,' she says. 'Through and through. You may think you're stardust, but it's really chance. We're like meat pies

– in the morning, flour, water, beasts eating grass, in the evening
– eaten; becoming excrement. Mismatches cobbled together,
worn, worn out.'

She shuffles through the papers on my table. 'Umar: the poet,
much afraid of death. Not fear of oblivion, but of judgement.
You? You've done nothing, Umar, not ventured from the shore
– not a line, a villanelle, a sonnet, even. Not a lemma, not a galaxy
identified. I'll give you something to be judged for.' And she
laughs.

'You're disappointed? That I'm not one of you, nor even one
of them? And maybe you aren't even one of you....' I say, taking
confidence.

'Disappointment's inappropriate,' she says. 'Regarding
anything. Luck, chance – are they the same? You must know
what track you're running on. And what did you propose to do,
if we'd not met on that short journey?'

'My wife's funeral – my partner, actually,' I say. 'I can't
marry anyone – no documents. I don't have my *bac*, so I'm on
the night shift. It's pretty slack: we'd drink dry martinis, but
we've no martini, so we drink the gin. I don't like the smell, but
that doesn't count as a disappointment.'

'You're young to have a dead wife,' she says, doubtful:
maybe with admiration. 'You're slippery. And you took a side
trip to avoid the burial. All too human, that.' She laughs. 'I don't
believe anything you say, but it's of no consequence, I'm sure.'

It's finished, buried. When she leaves, she says, 'Honour, like
duty – has no terminus. A bond, acknowledgment – an exchange
– of something, not of nothings, sweet or sour. Today will never
end – it's language, now: stored in your head. You can't get in to
scour it out!'

She rattles down the stairs – she's right. She never leaves.

*

'You're not a strong person, Umar. It can be attractive, but it makes you negligeable,' Farid says. 'There's lots like you in these countries they call rich, where they tell you you're protected. Everyone's supposed to be. But you don't understand what happens to you here, and don't understand the people who've fought every day, all their lives, to survive. I'd say – you are a species that's developed its own behaviour, and the rest, in combat every day, who live by expedients – are another. You can't distinguish aggression from intimacy; you're resigned to be a victim, so for no reason – you submit. You atone for people you despise – the slavers, exploiters, builders of empire with their holy books and guns. Trying to understand, accommodate – you act like a father, offering love – but really you're a stranger, a piece of flotsam: without value, unless you can be used, used even as a friend.'

'I know, Farid,' I say.

I mention Vinciane. He doesn't comment.

Later, he says, 'Too bad, you can't work in a circus – a freak, a sideshow. An innocent.'

'Everybody's sensitive, Farid,' I say. 'Up to a point. Me, like everybody.'

'Of course,' he says. 'But my point – that's the one you've missed. It isn't personal. You don't know how to deal with people more determined than you are.'

'You're right,' I say. 'If there is a whole, we don't know what it means, and if there *is* a meaning. And one another – a gesture, yours, what does it mean, and what does it mean to *me*? Religion leaves all the meaning outside your ken. Science? Everything's already there, someone set it up and switched it on – now 'identify the parts' the Someone says. Conside the Universe, probably no sideshow, though it's freaky through and through. Creation took some hours – what wastefulness – the galaxies, expansion ... and the fiddly parts, the worms, the microbes, atoms. Hit it with a hammer – and you've found a bomb! And what for? Are we here to puzzle it all out – a jigsaw with a trillion pieces, trillions of light-years wide? When done, it goes framed on Someone's wall. Good for creators, indifferent for us.'

'On the night shift, we can feel safe,' he says, pouring a dry gin for each. 'We're not protected, but we fill the gap, we're indispensable.'

*

A few days later, they close us down – night shift, day shift. All us irregulars are fired, same as the regulars, but they exist, we don't. Unexpected, except – I expected it. I expect everything.

I feel I must join a gang. They're being set up everywhere – an activity, an enterprise, a firm, a company, with its platoons. Trade, robbing, money factories. I disliked rules – now, they're all gone, it should be fantastic!

'You shouldn't take what happens, to you, around you, literally,' Farid says. 'It's like when they shout at you, 'Umar, go home,' when you are already here. I insist – what you have to do, don't take it as it seems – it isn't you. You'll back off, make a distance from what you see. Do what must be done, and disbelieve.'

'It's being inducted to a cult,' I say. 'Serving Shakti, a power never to be yours – one path leading to enlightenment, the other to success and dirty deeds. It takes your lifetime, and far far beyond.'

'You already have all the enlightenment there is,' says Farid, and he laughs. 'These cults, creeds, improvement or degradation – all a myth, illusion. We're always where we start, and don't know how or why we started there.'

*

Being, working, in a gang – is hard. They say it's easy; you have the power. It isn't really so. Some of the pots we have to scour – in big hotels – you stand inside them. Soups for giants? Sweet dark stuff that clogs a sewer. Cleaning the stables where they house the raptors. Fry them or their effluent? Goose green, *merde d'oie*: buckets of it. You are a parasite, you clean and pilot, and are eaten, consumed until all that's left's your life, still twitching like the lizard's severed tail.

The world of cleaning. '"The cleaning of the world", Farid. Every morning, it must be clean, the language too. Creation anew, the rubbish and the dirtiness – not shown in the prospectus. How long before I stop being a foot-soldier, cleaning; cleaning whole cities of their cinders, my own ashes inside my gut, I am my urn. I burned myself, quite smokeless – a lucent flame. In the urban forest with my rusty ax – extinguishing a species weak or past its time: in town, steam cannons, graders, jaws on vans – ever in full munch.

'How long – for ever? To become a manager! Give orders, get to use the language – "respect, honour, duty. Keep it clean!"

'Our behaviour too, we regulate. We're profligate and fuss. "don't pick that up, it's dirty, chuck it down, throw it away."

'You said my species – maybe just a sub, variety – would go extinct. One of those which choked, caught a disease, scratched the skin off, all of it, rashes and tumours.... Too delicate, too finicky, too ponderous with pondering.... So, do I have peers? Shall I miss them, or be missed? My dry brown skin, folded and crumpled in a drawer....'

We laugh. 'Look Umar,' he says, putting his sweaty face close up to mine – 'Don't be deluded. I am not your friend. I work alongside you, we share the dirty jobs – and that is it. I don't know, don't care, where you live, if you're alone or shacked: I don't ever want to know. You could sleep in the closet with the polishers, or in the cab – the JCB they use for heavy stuff – for all it interests me.

'We're military – we wear this sloppy uniform, that's never cleaned – our paradox! But all we do is shift the dirt, inert; it has no sentimental load. It's dumped. We gain some blasted territory, sweep it for mines – next day, the same. No one regrets the disappearance of exploded ordnance – no, they're glad. It means a day begins quite fresh and normally. Its past's been swept, incinerated. It is ash ... untagged civilians.

'No victory, no sting – just generations trudging till they go beneath the sod.

'There's guys in our trade that gets up every morning. and as usual there's been bombs – they pick the pieces up and put them in long bags. The camps – imagine cleaning those! Each day there's an inspection – if it's not whistle-white, they don't get cash for food. Imagine that, and imagine how your delicacy will make you disappear, like all the coloured birds, and animals that think they're fierce, but wear fur coats; and every winter – there's a cull! Kind nature, Umar! Gives you the long sleep!

'Believe there is a providence, believe what makes you glad! Tomorrow will be clean, just like today. The past, the day before – into the bag it goes ... Into the smell, the truck, the cruncher.'

I'm desperate. 'We have to get promoted, Farid,' I say. 'You are not my friend, ok, but being in a gang, there must be bosses, little ones, who tell the rest what they must do and then inspect, and handle cash and set the price....'

'Those cardamon seeds,' he says, 'You polish them, and I'll help you shovel out the mustard pots. Unless – we put the new stuff in on top. It's crust inside, but it will melt.'

'How they can eat!' I say. 'And leave so much exotic stuff – the manioc, the abalone grown in sheds....'

'It's poetry,' Farid says. 'The contrast, the variety. It makes us live, it's wheels – around they whirr, you rise and fall, like targets on a shooting stall....'

'You're fixed on circuses, Farid,' I say.

'There's everything,' he says. 'Abnormal strength and risk, precision – family. The raggedy beasts, that try to help, to understand ... the why of running endlessly around the ring. That was my world – my strong-man father, dead at 35 – exploded with the strain....'

'You're right, Farid,' I say. 'In this universe, there is no place for innocence. Nor gullibility. But if I'm honest with you: strength ... it's nothing. A triple somersault on to a single rope without a net or bungee, a once in a lifetime's spectacle, is nought. Every atom has a power immense ... hit it with a hammer: there's a bomb that finishes a city! Everything is curious – too detailed, too useless, or too powerful ... contagions lurking for a century that wake and gallop round the world like fire. A sense of humour is at work that thinks we're cretins, kills us in a hundred unexpected ways. Like outgrown toys. Dull pets.'

'Don't whine, don't pity yourself,' says Farid. 'You're the joke – enjoy it. It's true, I'm a better handler than you, and I'm giving up the broom and taking to the whip.

'I'll be your boss, but do just as I tell you, and nothing will have changed. Remember – what they call dirt is power.

'It's our life, and if you think it right, you're on the track to understanding. We eat dead flesh – wherever it has roamed alive. Fish fished up from primal minestrone, stuff brewed and coaxed from trees, made by insects or by frogs and snails, greens manured by sloths and boars, dusty blooms from compost heaps ... that's life, Umar, the core and kernel. Eat! Eat! The stranger it appears – the more it costs and better will it taste. Wisdom is there – distil it, clarify it: fluids. Excrescences. The source of life. Love the udders the gloop is teased from, the ropey tails that swish away the flies....'

We laugh. It's true. We eat the stuff, we drop it on the floor, sniff it, regurgitate and fart; it's us, it's ours, it drips from fornicating colibrì, we smear it on our lips and when the place is closed we cleaners sweep it up and bin it as the dawn – her rosy fingers bright with beetroot juice and paprika – marks the ending of our shift. The cycle done, we sleep like stiffs, and life goes on – eating and voiding, detritus abandoned everywhere by everyone; not to dwell on our coitus, decomposition, birthing, bleeding out....

'All the same, Farid,' I say. 'I'm pleased for you, that you're set over me. But all the same, I wish it had been me, requiring your obedience and fear.'

'Cut it!' he says. 'Some slacker didn't clean the mustard pots.... Do it! And into the tureen with you, Umar – then I'll put on the lid, it's bigger, shinier, than the sky – when you've polished it till you can see the stars, you can go down to the salt cellars, uncake the vents....'

Hospitality. We sell protection to them, and our bosses rip us off. We're theirs, they place us, but they take a cut. Farid is thief and bully. I must get out.

*

The train – the first step to escape. I take care Vinciane's not in view. The idea – that even when we meet, like snooker balls that kiss and travel on – we have a duty to each other, one we must evaluate – it's wonderful. A gateway.

'Do you mind?' the woman, Saodat, enquires, as she sits next to me. 'You mustn't mind – I'm curious, inquisitive. You may be prejudiced about me, but I'll tell you anything you want – and you the same.'

For sure, there is a con that comes in at the end of this. You wander into someone's poverty and need: to get away, you have to play a higher card – your greater poverty, more need. It's humiliating, and you can't avoid.

'All these people!' she begins, looking round. 'All different, you'd be sure there'll be a war, or rioting. People from everywhere, in communities, all coloured differently, worshipping different stars. Packing pistols, spitting out the window. Language disputes, and rapes ... at the very least....'

'It's because we are the same there's wars,' I say. 'People don't use language – they shop: and trade insults. Words are mere gestures – you use signs and grunts. We're all polyglots in that.'

'Yes,' she says. 'We're both right. It's good to meet a person who has thought. Has reached the understanding....'

I'm flattered. I think of Vinciane, and honour. I'm on the path to know what that involves. This woman, who'd immediately told her name, must be aware that revelation can take decades, or a flash. I'm somewhere in between.

'We know everything,' I say, becoming expansive, confidential, 'because we're part of it. You can fight that knowledge forever as a sceptic, or it comes wholly unexpected, when you are in lotus position, or running from the cavalry. Everything – is simple. Knowing that doesn't give it meaning, beyond what it is, it appears. You know, that's all – the whole. It's the parts that take technique and training to master – repoussé work is hard, I'm told. Illuminating texts....'

'My!' she says, 'You *are* extravagant. And all you know – is by hearsay! You know nothing by yourself, nothing of you, of me....'

'I'm not a pure being, Saodat,' I say.

I tell her, editing, about Vinciane ... as if the train could be a train of thought, or circumstance, coincidence. A place of meeting that must signify?

'No,' says Saodat. 'It's just you're very limited. No horizon, no resistance and moreover – you're not free. You can't enjoy. You are suspicious, but you fall for any lies. A little fascist, possibly?'

'Rubbish,' I say, starting to think of spinning her a tale. 'My work has been to clear it – from mountains, glaciers, volcanic spates, a Ganges or an Everest ... using utensils from the devil's scullery.... Imagine! – a *bain marie* that holds two Marys, one prissy and one naughty, both needing grace and welfare .... My gargantuan employment....'

She smiles, not listening. 'I see your aimlessness,' she says, touching my knee. 'It hurts me – seeing you inflating your environment, hoping its energy will pass to you, and swell you up. And yet, for me, you're perfect. What I'm looking for – for what I plan, is you. Not "you specific", but an ordinary, drifting, struggling man. A person, that is. Without gender: without qualities. A simpleton, who grasps the universe, because the universe is all he has. Someone who'll do anything, because he thinks it changes what he is, and opens up new worlds, new panoramas. Vanity, my friend. You're in denial: you understand the universe, and yet you think that if *you* change, it changes everything ... primarily the universe. Changes from chaos into order, malevolence to sympathy. Think a moment. You're wrong, you'll see you're wrong – but don't despair. I could bring you something new, while all the rest remains the same. Including you.'

'It's a paradox,' I say. 'What's true in it – is hard to swallow.'

'When we're about to die,' she says, 'we understand. Being, or not. There, not there ... It goes for you, and goes for the universe. The only change – the presence of the negative. Quite trivial, but experienced as drastic.

'Take heart! Some understand this long long before the final day, and live quite tranquilly.'

The con? Maybe the story in itself. Like a dancer with a scarf, who weaves a wonderful solo, unaccompanied, and disappears – and there's the scarf, that goes on dancing, in her form.

*

'I need a helper,' Saodat says. 'Literate, incurious. Does what he's told and gives advice, but is not hurt when it's ignored.'

It's true, I think: one thing does not explain another thing. Nothing coheres, or follows on. Something happens – not a precedent. No pattern, no design.My fleeting tale with Vinciane – not even sordid, just a nothing, that leaves a concept, burrowing, worming, as if a wormhole made a depth, not just a void. Qualities? Intangible? It leaves – a nothing, a hole too small for you to go down it and explore. It's entered by a worm – out flies quite something else – a tiny bird....

*

Saodat has an office in the city. It's very clean. No need for me to clean again. There's only us two, and I'm an expert in not leaving dirt. Or, rather, in leaving and removing it.

'Now, tell me the idea, Saodat,' I say. 'Working here – do I need a uniform? Am I paid by the week or by the day, the hour? How will you measure work – does work mean "presence", or doing some activity?'

She ignores me – that's part of work she does, as boss. 'Little countries,' she begins. 'Scrunched, confned, compressed. Between mountains, rivers, bits of desert no one wanted, pieces of in-between, of scrub or coast, folds in a map, places where they'd run out of flags to plant.... Places full of dispute: disparate people – or, all the people lookalikes – unique, not integrated ... a language no one wants to learn or write a grammar for....

Religion improbable, an epic disproportionate.... Either too much like the people in big countries, losing specificity: or tiny enclaves of identicals....'

I interrupt. 'Everywhere's like that, or is a mixture of both kinds,' I say. 'You ought to drop the idea of country. That's what I'd do. Start again. Or leave things as they are – but not as categories. "Small"? It's silly....'

She's enraged. 'No! You haven't understood. There will be an association of those places, because you haven't grasped – they're *small*.'

'Well, go ahead,' I say. 'There's those republics in the Russian Federation – big or small? Desert countries – huge, with almost no one settled in them....'

She stares at me. Why can't I follow her?

'It may be ridiculous,' I say. 'But perhaps you're right. Lots of countries, disparate, can get together, swap and trade, get hugger-mugger – other places never solve disputes! They suffer conflict, ostracism – can't co-exist with their minorities, appease their separatists. Then, you might say – there's everlasting questions that affect the world, all have an interest in settling them: migrants, famine, catastrophes. No answer, always improvised or just ignored. Maybe "small countries" will seem quite plausible, worth signing up for if you feel....'

'I've my title,' Saodat says. '"President". And the cash. There's clubs of indigenes, of islands – those do well .... so, mine will work....'

'The point is adding yours to what exists,' I say. 'Will it attract, what will it do?'

'You find a road,' she says, 'And walk along it. As you go, companions join you. They know where the road goes, where the brigands and the check-points are. That's how the future works, Umar. If it weren't so, the future and the past would be identical. A story is like this, and you're a character.'

'I see how dwarves of different origin might get together, not quibbling over millimeters of a cut-off height,' I say. 'Tall people, come to that. The ugly and the beautiful ... they'd self-select, be a movement, split and fight ... pay dues, have drinks....'

'We're like that,' Saodat says. 'The species loves variety, extremes. It loves complaining, settling disputes, it loves conformity and moderation. I promise you, Umar, we fit – you and I, my idea and yours.'

'It isn't what I want, or care about,' I say, seeming to sulk, but really, I despair. It's a cage.

'See if your gang will take you back,' she says. 'After they've punished you, a life of cleaning flatware.... And here's a puzzle that will last you all your life – what corrupts more, money, or not having it?'

'If it's a puzzle,' I say, 'even banal, it means I'm outside it, trying to piece an answer together. Though in this case, there is none.'

'There is for me,' says Saodat, 'There has to be.'

*

We make a peace. 'Each is right and wrong,' she says. 'You'll see. The little countries lack variety. Resources are precarious – but all of them must feed and trade, grow, and assert themselves.'

It's true. The little countries – they sign up to have a peek at how the others manage. Cash circulates.

Saodat – where has she gone? She leaves a note – 'Don't make it seem we're taking cash. We must be clean....'

We are, I am, at least. There's not much work, and I'm not paid much for doing it. Saodat – I never see her, and our conversation on the train is the beginning and the end of all our interchange.

Saodat sends another note – how she is moving on, bigger countries, more direct responsibilities. They considered me to take her place, she says, but after all – they want a person of a higher calibre.... 'Your past as vagrant hasn't helped', she says.

It's clear I know the secrets – the finance, the conflicts, the repressions and the plans – 'Of course, you have the oath of secrecy ... a breach of trust would follow you and you would pay, but you have a sense of honour, and it's your duty to respect the confidentiality of what you learn at work....'

If you are paid by someone, you must expect they'll threaten you ... 'pay back what you have spent, or keep your silence' ... perhaps in what remains of your dim and cloudy life, you'll leak – some drizzle, April showers of secrets, scandals.... It's not worth your while.

Silence. Neither credit nor discredit. As with Vinciane.

I remember Saodat. 'Life is messages and information, and it's up to you to pass the revelation on, to choose the acolytes, to be one of the enlightened ones. Or ... you can believe the messages and truth are meant for you alone, your secrets. Either way, to be authentic, what is yours must be also everyone's. They're transparent. There are no secrets in the world – if you reveal yours, or keep them to yourself, what difference does it make? The secrets have been known and written down for many

many lifetimes. A secret doesn't mean it is unknown or new. By definition, it's been known, passed on....'

Does it carry duties? It all depends – on something. Not on me, not on you.

Some people you don't see again, and that is what they want, and so do you. No one is owed – you have been dumped, or else you fled.

It's hard to start again, that's all. Dodge those from the past, the gang. Cadge some employment.

Saodat's investigated for theft – does she protect me? She didn't cut me in. Her world is up above mine – I fell out of the balloon. Maybe never climbed into the basket.

She owes me, and probably, I owe her. Every country owes her something – what, I don't know, and she's priced that in, for sure, although you can't.

These women, appearing unsummoned, inconcluding, disappearing – with a criticism, an exhortation ... my failure to grasp duty, my 'vagrancy', vagabondage, that seems enforced, unwanted and resented, yet becomes an obstacle to respect or advancement.... I seek them for an explanation, and also seek to avoid them, to avoid another meeting.

Things mustn't, surely, just happen to you: there must be something to understand, to learn from, even when you know it all. *Especially* when you know it all – if you learn Russian, that's not the end! You can't say – 'I know that language, so, that's the end of it. Finished.'

You are in movement, alive – so, there must be a destination, mustn't there?

There's hobos and there's peasants, those forever on the road, and those pinned forever to the land. They distrust each other, but nomads, the in-betweens, they're hated universally. There's not many things that each of us can do and be.

Adventure: that's worth seeking out!

*

'I'm naive and ill-informed,' I say.

'I know,' says Tito.

'Tito' comes from Titus, not Yugoslavia. With Saodat, he was a go-between, a lobbyist, a curious. He hung around.

'I seem to be condemned,' I say. 'A vagabond.'

Tito's expansive.... 'In this country, there's agents in transit,' he says. 'It's an exaggeration to say they're 'secret'. I saw an acquaintance, in his hotel room, take from his case what looks like a toy, a space gun. It's part of a guided missile system he's trying to sell on. This was all years ago – no one said a word against liberation. The people needed to be freed – freedom in Africa, freedom everywhere. Money was needed, and everyone here was poor, or said they were. Real money passed over everybody's heads. Huge sums were sent abroad to safety. It is stolen, in a way, but though it's to guarantee an exile in luxury, it's also to buy support for an entourage, a court in waiting; to finance an improbable return when you've been overthrown – the old regime, buying new power. And while you are in exile, you need protection. You have to pay off – not bad guys, but a state, probably a bad state – so they don't give you trouble.'

'It's opera,' I say. 'The smugglers' chorus.'

'The bodies were real,' he says. 'There was no final curtain and no resurrections.

'This country, full of people who were Lenin, or Lenin and Trotsky both, Peter the Painter, Stalin and Truman simultaneous, pacifists with guns, internationalists in someone's pay.... A macedonia of species, of variants, intrigues, and hybrids. If you had a political past of threat or terror, you could disappear here. You were a drop of water in a rolling stream; no one can keep track of leaves on trees, they fall quite regularly and are replaced by others absolutely different and identical.'

'And me?' I ask. 'This is all long ago. Those people were professional – now, all is changed and changing too.... It's improvised and amateur, ingenuous, unpaid.... And yet – there's stalking, persecutions....'

'I work for a regime,' says Tito. 'You wouldn't like it, nor do I, but it's in history, and so am I, and if I step outside the history, I'll never work again and maybe go to jail or to the morgue. Cash for arms, and arms for cash – that is the tale.

'At the time, I'd not taken it too serious. Kadhafi, for example – he had had lots of cash. Everyone was after it. He financed everything, himself as well. It was well-known: cash was needed everywhere, for anything. Only a few were prepared to care where it came from. Not me. I was very young. I was a liberal – extreme: a democrat – extreme. An anarchist, through being soft and ingenuous and passionate.... I joined everything, always for the cause. Money, flight, arms – bungs and agents, mercenaries and helicopters – it was all there and visible, stage furniture. Stage machinery: the crude shady tools you need to set the people free.

'The cause was everything. I didn't care how. I still don't care too much.

'They put me on a list. I was on a list, unknowing, unsuspecting, and stayed on it when I had no more interest in politics. I knew the history of everywhere, the old exhausted guys, their causes dessicated, traduced. Old thieves, assassins, a few saintly ones, on icons.

'I didn't know I had a brand, scorched into me, a place I couldn't see, a crude symbol, carried for life, a smell of burn, of flesh cooked and cauterised.

'That list's the strongest force internationally – stronger than globalisation, than rich and poor, than viruses or cash. However much you change, you won't get off, not ever. If you're desperate, someone will pay for you to spy, for or against somebody, and some principle or against it. You need money, lots of it, by then; you'll never see it, but the need is there.'

I can't respond. I feel a dread....

He's done his act: he stands back, interested to see how it's gone down. How much is true?

'None of this is true, don't believe it, even if you see the documents, it's all false,' he goes on, not registering that I'm there, in front of him. 'The themes change, the big intelligences reassert themselves, but cash that you won't see is still the wheels beneath the carriage. Everything you hear is true, sometimes you have to turn it inside out.

'Now, it isn't liberation that's the word. The sparking-plugs are different: food, corruption, and religion. Climate, health? – Intelligence isn't interested in what affects the species – its concern is keeping order, constituted orders that it's told it must sustain. Sometimes – creating a disorder is the way – it isn't up to you to judge, probably not up to anyone. Show interest, join, sign, or read – associate with someone who does any one of those, or has a grudge against you ... you're on the list, you're under watch....'

'I'm sure you're right,' I say. 'But tell about the list. That's what is interesting. You say I might be on it, never will get off – that it will affect me all my life, my work, my friends, my fortune....'

'Not so,' says Tito. 'Your fortune's what it is because you are inadequate. But yes, you're on the list. You get put on, you can't get off, or verify anything I've said....'

'Well, Tito,' I say, despairing. 'What side are you on?'

'Accept,' he says. 'It's like being born – the wrong class, colour, faith or none at all. It's if you are lefthanded – so the doors and cans don't open for you. If you've kids, they're on the list, like when there were bad fairies at their birth.'

'There must be a way back,' I say. 'Making redress. Clarifying what you were, and how you change.'

*

Obligations – you collect them, owe, without response. Debts collected without ever seeing cash. The involuntary – the universe is based on action and reaction. All the rest seems fortuitous. Somewhere, there's a will; something must be voluntary? And yet – it's not.

*

'You're an innocent,' says Tito. 'So I won't ask you to do dirty trips.'

'I'm not sure,' I say. 'I don't want to settle down, since you offer me a heavy load.... I'd like to meet someone with a personality instead of quips. What kind of trips, anyway?'

'The carrying things and meeting people kind of work,' says Tito. 'As for which side you're on – personalities will make it clear to you, as you jog by.'

'I expect it's like all work,' I say, angling for information. 'It's dull until you're caught.'

'Risk is what you need,' says Tito, handing me a heavy suitcase. 'Look back. Your awful normal life. Hop hop – like a scared bird, from retreat into defeat! Concentrate, Umar. Reflection and hesitancy – sheer nullity. It doesn't mean a thing.'

My world is full of Farids. They sit in the plane, in whatever seat I have, they're next to me. They chat. They tell me they are thieves and bullies, proud of it. What am I? On the way to being thief. Then I'm sure I'll manage bullying.

*

'You're like mafia,' says Aboubacar, 'You agents. But you're viewed with less respect. True, the mafiosi – if they disappear, no one looks for them, to help them out. You're different – embarrassing.

If you're lost, there is an incident; they look for you, intrusively, suspicious.

'Here – we kept the white room that you've wanted all your life. You can stay here....'

It's so. The beams are white, the floor tiles too, powdery, like talc, and the sun .... at midday you see nothing but the white, and in the fields, beyond the souk, there's ospreys, or they could be plastic bags, caught by a breeze, and lifting up, displacing; there's a line of green, a thread of water.

'We kept this room for an infinity,' says his ancient partner, Tabby. 'Everyone we knew has left. Lots were expelled. Kadhafi skewered like an underdone kebab. Liberation days are gone. We kept the room this perfect white, not for tradition, but for rockers, for modernity. It must come, by logic and the will. Instead – there's you. You're not a mod? And not a rocker?'

'I hadn't really wondered. But I think you're right,' I say. She brings me food – white, sweet – a plate of lokum. It makes me gag. I always hoped to end up here – instead, it seems an end for these two ancients, their skin stretched taut to splitting point across the face they seem to share.

It's reasonable, but they're wrong – modernity should come, here too, but it doesn't, or if this is it, you wouldn't want it, wouldn't want to long for it, the next chapter, even if you're still a character, belong to the plot, fading out, but full of commentary, even some conclusions.

'The problem is,' says Aboubacar, 'We were prepared. But no one listened to us. And we heard nothing.'

'You didn't know what you were waiting for, or what must be lost to make a space for it,' I say. 'For me, this is protection, but I don't know what against.'

'You idiot!' screams Tabby, hopping up and down like a crow in spate – 'Protection is indifferent. It recognises nothing accidental. That is the point – you're protected against everything. That's why you shouldn't leave, or you won't live to make a second trip.'

'Tito said it wouldn't be a dirty deal,' I say.

'It's not, it's not,' shouts Tabby. 'It's that you'll be taken, no one will know where, you won't return, or reappear with green and golden shoes with curly points, at your belt a snickersnee.'

'Believe me, Umar, we get heated up because we care for you,' says Aboubacar, stroking my arm. 'What Tabby says is true as true. Here you are, upon the earth: there's nothing dirty – every day we clean the room. It's clean as clean, and that's the end. Ends are like that. Mostly, we are pleased they come and there is no way back. Start is for once: go back, it's not a start, it's repetition.'

'So, where I am,' I say, 'is a re-reading. Not a post-station.

'I'm still unclear – is "here" about me, or about you? You're settled, but I'm not, I am precarious, it seems....'

'Correct,' he says. 'There is no rest. You can't avoid the views, but they are never part of you, there is no link – you move, and you won't know what happens in them. Do they change? Perhaps. It's of no significance to you.'

'Then I might as well be gone,' I say. 'It seems inevitable.... You don't give me rest, my questioning ... slides past us all.'

'That room,' Tabby says, looking rejuvenated, calm as a rock, 'It's good you think it's just for you. We remember it as our tent. The tent was white, the sheep as well. You know why we're not still there – us shepherds?' She doesn't wait for my evasive guess. 'Spies and trouble. And a fad.... They, the people, started eating sheep. It was intolerable – from textiles into joints.... A massacre. Disgusting.'

'It must have been far far back,' I say: it isn't credible. Sheep ribs and eggs and thin unleavened bread: a classic – the shepherds are the first to eat their charges....

'We're not like that,' says Aboubacar. 'You could stay in the room, the tent. There is no carpet; you can't provide. You've no fleece. You're cropped, maybe even – bald. It's a poor future, but you should be safe....'

He holds my hand, squeezes it hard. I might be safe? He loves me, possibly, useless as I am, not providing wool or any useful thing. Not sheep-shape. Best to be off, though.... It's harsh and arid all around ... a dried-out oasis. The souk – persil and batteries.

Tabby hugs me, kisses me, her tears run down my face. I feel the urge to weep with her – but why? These are my shields, and my defenders. They've been my refuge. 'My son,' she says. 'My poor son.'

I leave the heavy suitcase with them, and move on. The souk is empty, people have gone to pray, or maybe just – they've gone. It's very hot. No one is buying at this hour.

The order of the spheres and their movements through the six directions, north, south, east, west, up, down, constitutes a primary coordinate system within which all creation is situated. All traditional sciences share this common frame of reference and, because of this commonality, manifest an integration basic to all the creations of society. (Nader Ardalan and Laleh Bakhtiar, The sense of unity)

The quote – Tito's 'Note for Travellers' – is stuck to the ticket 'for unlimited distances' – the envelope has my name superimposed on others. We expect that; just as, if we're curious, we spy. If we're not curious – why did we come? Death, as Tabby said, is the only way out.

*

All sheep are good – you need to watch the shepherds, though. Ah, these precepts! How banal!

It all coheres, by definition: unity.... Like an aeroplane – there's nothing outside but a void – and yet, open the wrong door, all is sucked out, a kite's tail of similars, ancestors too, ending in a mash anonymous, falling and flying, hand in hand and shouting out, all of us possessed with what must happen next, even a totem from the hold tumbling, colliding, with the tiny phials of booze, world food joining in the universal fall – a streamer of asparagus, little potatoes like a rope of yellowing pearls, down to the resolution ... a chain gang landing naked in a field of sheep....

Tito – I never want to see him, and it's all a secret, where we are, my contract, and my pay. I can't ask about the suitcase, where I left it. If I did wrong? No one will know – it's capital in bundles, perhaps, or laser cannons that can blind – what goes silent round the world....

There'll be new orders.

I always miss my destiny by fingertips. Not only my objectives: mankind's agenda. Transfiguration – never quite in reach, the destinations promised, threatened – not available.

True, cleaning the crocks was hell.

Tabby and Aboubacar should have brought me paradise, but what could be mine is left in waiting for something they won't want.

The rest is neither here nor there: just inconclusive. Little pleasure to be had. Everything's a lesson, if you want; might give a clue to what next time you should expect.

Tito is invisible, inaudible. Sometimes there are futile errands – a box, a folder. As if the shape meant you are in motion, bearing despatches from the avant-garde, the elementary School of Paris, to a new cutting up and reassembling of the body – the body politic. The cube, the collage.

This is Vinciane's honour, duty.

Is it?

It's a paradox. Spies see nothing; they don't know what they see. I saw no honour, had no duty. A pigeon, a stooly, I couldn't bend to read the message tied to my leg. Easier than working in secret for a state is working for a multitude of states. They won't pay. Besides, you're betting on all horses in the race – a tyro.... an idealist believing in all ideals at once, whatever they might be, all that are supposed to divide up the world.

*

'I thought I wanted truth and freedom. But really – I wanted them for myself alone. I had no idea of what they meant for a society, a generality. I chose isolation, not splendid, but to dig my hole, and have others throw me into it. I thought the system persecuted me, and mainly me – really, what damaged me was my weakness, my very own.

'The system was something I leapt into, and complained when it tore off my skin. I ignored the rest of those who suffered as I did – not even privileging my own pain over theirs, but puffing it up till it was bigger than the sodden clouds that fill the sky.'

'Then there's nothing that can be done for you,' my neighbour says. 'You've managed it again – the truth is truth about yourself, that there's nothing to be done for you, nothing you can do for yourself, no one in your situation you might reassure. Your remedy, your cure – is to describe in detail all your symptoms, all your disease. You're a pathology, through and through.'

'I don't know what to do,' I say. 'We all know what to do, and can't do it.'

'It's lucky you're not trustworthy,' he says. 'So you won't get to do anything significant.'

'If you need help,' I say, 'you can't rely on me, but I'll do what you say.'

'You seek an outlet for your troubles, my poor friend,' he says. 'I wouldn't trust the humans with you, but I have an urgent need. The Westerlies. They blow in birds, mostly the huge ungainly ones – with broken wings and broken compasses. Flamingoes, hoopoes ... even the tiny bulbuls – those spend the night carousing, then they're plucked up, storm-tossed, into the spirals, round they gyre – and then ... it's calm: they're dumped. We pick them up. The eagles, storks and cranes – some vultures, swept up from death-watch, reach my haven....'

'Rest and recreation – like us all, that's what they need,' I say. 'It's not at all what I had hoped. There is no mystery, and no reward. More cleaning, that's the word that makes me shudder and I would reject it out of hand....

'Birds. They live above us, in the sky – and yet, they're limited. They need our help – the flightless ones, they languish, disappear. The big ones, seven metres tall – are skeletons in drawers and showcases.'

He looks at me, a steady gaze, a tear not far away ... I can't share his passion or his grief. His case says 'Axel'. A trademark, possibly.

'Axel,' I say, 'give me a life. A room, at least. I'll do the job. And – what I suffer isn't being weak, it's being curious. I get too close, so as to see what will ensue.'

'Well,' he says. 'In this instance, you did well. A keeper in a cage.'

*

Axel is a thoughtful type, who's read, and, as an amateur, has looked all round the text, the underside, the secret drawer.

'What do you think of error, Umar?' he asks. 'Your famous namesake, or his English ghost – his poetry is full of the unexpected, the anomalous. Error? You see, Voltaire made clear the basis of our civility, our multifolded, multicoloured civilisation. Tolerance, Umar – rests on the possibility, the probability, of error. We make mistakes, there is nothing, no one, that's infallible. That is our ground. Error. Mistake. We tolerate because we're fallible. That's what our rights, our honour, duty, our democracy – rest on. The motto is – "We may have got it wrong." A little or a lot, everything or a quibble. It's the flaw, Umar, in the crystal, in the bowl. The flawed messiah, gets it wrong – and so, and so.... First him, then us. The firmament – it cracks. From side to side – you recognise the quote? And have you ever been tasked with observance of a right, a duty – and you've never known: whose is the fault. Yours? The accuser's? Or just the ground of being, the way things are: the ever-present possibility: the mistake?'

'It's ingenious,' I say, thinking of Vinciane: what's done, not done, present and future, the act of intercourse, a kind of sacrament, of being in the world ... or even not.

'These birds,' says Axel, 'made the mistake. They took off, were dismasted in the heavens, landed here – some die. Your colleague, Alicia – she is trained. She does triage, and many you don't see, and wouldn't want to, she despatches. The one that can be cured – she passes on. The rest ... in peace.'

He opens up a box. It's full of tails and crests, breasts and wings. Is that a Carolina Parakeet – though extinct, and here a shining corpse. She should have died in 1938, the very last ... the Little Blue Macaw? She's here: she ought not be. There's ocellated turkey feathers, quetzals galore, the military macaw – echoes of Chiapas, the Tupinamba' featherworkers – here's a scarlet ibis, how the Tupi plumists loved them.... As do I, and yet ... all dead, most from the Americas, others from islands long ago that sank; the last parakeet on the last palm, a desolate ensign....

Axel shuts the trunk.

'You see,' he says. 'Mistakes. Those, we live by, and these birds....'

'They died from their mistake,' I say.

'Yes,' he says. 'That's how you see the world. You fear your death too much, Umar, it doesn't mean you won't have one, soon or late – maybe,' and he chuckles, 'from a mistake.'

'It makes sense, Axel,' I say. 'But answers nothing, no questions.'

'Yes,' he says, 'It's like Alex, Alex the grey. They taught it to communicate. So what? Imagine one of us, one person – can communicate with other species.... It would be up to them to explain to that intelligent, benighted one, to expound everything, about the individual. The representative, the soul, the spirit: there, right there, on its perch or in our armchair.... Where he, she, stands, the history, the interaction.

'It's like – 'Alex,' we say, 'you are a parrot. Tell us all.' 'No,' Alex says, 'I may be what you say – and what are parrots? What are they to me? If I am one of them, what difference does it make, to them, to me? What is our history? Our purpose? Am I dead, alive, or hanging on – a frozen egg? What does our existence *mean* to us, to you, to anyone?'

'You see, saving these wrecked creatures needs no reasoning. I don't need justify. They made mistakes, is all; it is enough. We set them on their legs, their wings, and off they fly. Some don't. All the rest, for us – is ignorance. And probably for them – they're opportunists, just like us. They have a parliament of fowls, it's said – and we don't bother with their polity, we read their entrails, watch if they fly to left or right. And when we see it doesn't matter, not a bit – we just abandon magic. In a twink. They are a mystery, Umar, as you know. We sense in them there is a little piece of us, ourselves – a shred of reciprocity. That's all – the rest is all adventure, speculation. But we, and only we, invent the mysteries. They're what we do not know.'

'And yet,' I say, 'Tolerance, the big mistake, or rather, the big consequence of a mistake – is here. My casual encounter.... That leaves me wondering – do I owe? A boss corrupt – do I denounce, or do I hide myself?'

'Oh please,' he laughs. 'No sordid stories, please! Decide what qualities you want to bear, and set about acquiring them! Who, what, is your duty, what happens if you slink away? No anecdotes, I beg!'

He hands me rolls of notes. I start to count them – 'Don't do that!' he shouts. 'I never make mistakes – besides, what's there's exactly right.'

The work's rewarding: wear a helmet, and you're fine. Alicia is delightful, though I don't make a move. She spends the days plucking the birds she's had to kill, putting the feathers in the trunk.

'Alas,' she says, 'The Incas went extinct before I could make a feather cape and crown for some big cheese. Maybe they'll come again, if we prepare a habitat....'

'Oh fiddle, Alicia,' Axel says, laughing hugely. 'We wouldn't understand them if they came!'

I hear she lives with Hakim, an elderly gentleman – I imagine him, a yellow cheroot aglow, a hookah at the ready.... I share my image with Axel, who laughs.

'Hakim is a Lear's Macaw,' he says. 'Rare, frail, chained to his perch. A greater love, reciprocal, for anyone I've never seen.... Beware, dear Umar, don't dare to be an Icarus. No risk, and no mistake – walking the earth, in chastity, is task enough for us.'

*

'Axel feels nothing for the birds,' Alicia says. 'He likes doing what they say is good, that's all. I like Hakim – otherwise, this is a crap job, dirty work – so it's good you like the birds, Umar, I guess.'

'Oh,' I say, surprised, 'I don't like work, but I've done lots of it. I trust to chance, not luck, or liking. You could say it's an experiment, making your fortune, like you're supposed. Remember the goose game, the *gioco dell'oca*. You could pay your way, going from hostelry to hostelry, winning and cheating – except it isn't legal. No one plays. In fact, you cannot cheat. It doesn't matter, not a bit. It isn't luck, nor chance – it's fear of cheating, gambling to make some people really poor. I don't agree that everything comes down to chance – there must be a place for errors too. That's what's allowed: mistakes. The rest is rules, been there for ever, except we don't know what they are, and there's this pretence it's wonderful to discover them, find what's behind – the everything. Behind, inherent: a design or just the happenstance. But knowing the formulas – it doesn't change a thing. The idea is. "You can't cheat chance. That is, you mustn't.""

'That doesn't seem quite right,' Alicia says, but I don't stop.

'Using the transport. Sitting near someone, who by chance,' I say, roaming through my memory '... It gives you life, a story. It searches you out, and makes you sweat, despair, tarnish and burn. But – that's the point. To set out, travel, take the chances given to you – make the mistake, the big one, even way back, at the start or usually before.... That's it! Nothing to do with birds at all.'

We laugh.

Alicia throws armfuls of grey feathers in the trunk. 'Axel was mayor – an island full of slaves and canes,' she says. 'The men did the harvest, lived on the cash till the next year. They gathered in the square, everybody round to cheer them on, and then the bosses said they wouldn't pay – some guys said they'd done the work, and maybe they had not. There'd be investigations.... Then came the rage ... the heat ... the hate....

'The guys sang the Carmagnole, and everyone joined in, and Axel told the owners to pay up, pay anyone who asked – "Or else in an hour, we'll all be dead. You, me, the guys who did and didn't work, the cops, your goons, the people in the square. There is no choice – do good...."

'And in the end they did; the magnates paid. Two thousand people sang the Carmagnole, Axel says. Afterwards, he was chased out, and that was when he had the inspiration of the birds. And that's why you and me are here, and Axel too.'

*

There's Westerlies and Northerlies. Hakim dies, and Alicia leaves – we don't get a parting kiss.

Axel pays me Alicia's share as well as mine, and I give death, and life. The world shrinks like a football losing air. The winds blow strong – there's rooks, thrown from their nests by night.

'I can leave at any time,' says Axel. 'I understand – this work won't end, it will increase and never stabilise....'

'It's success,' I say. 'Success always means more than you can cope, it does for you, it finishes by breaking up and so there's no more room for you.'

'I leave it all to you,' says Axel. 'At least – those island guys, they got their pay, so the next year they could bring the harvest in.'

The winds bring in the birds, they look like storm-broken deckchairs on a beach. Axel removed the feather-trunk – I close the cage, scatter the food – manna on the earth.

*

'Umar,' says my new friend, Tuan. 'Are you still living? Once, heaven and hell were obscure places, much talked about, but

needing poets to write about them. Now, anyone can live there –
will live in one, or both, in prose.'

'Mine's a caliph's name,' I say. 'It doesn't mean I am a
terrorist, or even that I have a faith. I don't want to mention work
– it's there all the time, like weather. You can't avoid it, but it
changes. Most work you get is underpaid, so you can move on,
and no one cares at all. The more you're paid, the more servile
you have to be, making rules the others do not follow. You start
inventive, but soon you spend your life in court....'

'You've had an easy life,' says Tuan. 'Some of us walked out
of where we lived or took a dinghy. We won't go back. Those
who walked were lucky – others ran or crawled.

'Forget the caliphs – reflection went from comedy divine to
human comedy: always closer to the earth. And then, no one was
laughing; comedy was over. For a tragedy – do you need a poet?'

'Ah!' I say, starting to think how Tuan's sounding shallow.
'You don't need pause for answers, Tuan – you have your
response prepared....'

'The serious stuff,' he says, changing register – 'It's floating
on the top, along with all the other scum. Who cares? It's become
trivial, I fear. Or – maybe I should say "I'm pleased it has".'

'It's inconclusive, Tuan,' I say, 'and it will always be, until
the last.'

We're moving fast.

'I dislike asking, Tuan,' I say, 'Since we're going rapidly, and
soon we'll be off this craft and back into our lives. But....'

'I'm always looking for obedience,' he says, 'Without
pretensions, so when they're fired, they don't complain.'

'You mean people,' I say, 'Anyone. I see you dodge work issues; race, class, gender, all that stuff: the history. But.... What...? Your angle?'

'Public philosophy,' says Tuan. 'I get invites. I enthral. I have credit – same as, but better than, having wealth.'

'Accommodation too?' I ask.

'I have a base out east,' he says. 'I'm the modern thing. I go around the world, bearing my gift, and to those back there, it's as if I carry something fresh. It isn't so. I'm of a piece. I've worked out what I say, it doesn't change. I have my interests too, material ones – study and cure, accommodate and learn. Bricks and glass, Umar.'

'And to what end?' I ask. 'Illumination? Or revelation? A bigger light-bulb or – the invention of new energy?'

'I have a little army too,' he says, quite coy. 'Believers. Simple, honest types. Nothing mystical. But, Umar, I'm afraid – I have no vacancy.'

'What is it you are after, Tuan?' I ask, disappointed, not surprised.

'Oh,' he smiles. 'You could come, observe. Lots do. Eat and sleep for free. Don't be afraid – I need defending. I don't attack. I'm after truth, the real – like everyone.'

'It sounds terrifying,' I say. 'All that stuff. Piled up, mortared together.'

'You're the frightening one, Umar,' he says. 'You're the only sighted blind man I have come across. Trust the air, the wind. That is vital, without those, you suffocate.'

'The wind's a killer, Tuan,' I say, thinking of the storks. 'I'm not sure at all, that truth and the real is what I want. I think, rather, that I don't. I'm sure to get to those, you have to understand, to justify, accept – and try to reason round. If I come as an observer to your stage – it's because I'm racked with thirst and hunger. You offer me the empty bowl, and say it will be filled. How? By you? By me? It's important I should know....'

'Well, here we are,' says Tuan, not amused. 'Take your empty bowl and follow me. You can carry things, and call a cab – the buildings are so tall in this dull place, there's eternal twilight in the streets. It's home....'

And that is true, and real – he's right.

'No one has ever escaped what's going to happen to them,' he says, as we get in the car.

*

The believers are not doers, so I get to do a job not offered, didn't want.

Tuan chivvies me – I remember Saodat, and regret her absences. Tuan checks us every hour.

'How big is this army?' I ask Poirette, who shares my desk.

Alicia knew the calls of hundreds – birds would acknowledge her at first, then stayed schtum. It could have been the accent. I called her the Senmurgh, the bird that is a thousand birds, that's pictured, never seen, and tastes delicious roasted, though no one's ever tasted her. And – it's flightless too, like her. Poirette, instead, has no skill, no doubts. I insist, 'A division? A brigade? Cavalry or camel corps? And why?'

'There's always persecutions,' Poirette says. 'The Baha'i, the Yazidi. Hurons. Sioux. All kinds of warrior. People's beliefs and claims. Standing out. It's best to be prepared.'

'But Tuan's the bird of wisdom, Poirette,' I say. 'The others give the speech, and he comes on and sums it up, gets the applause. He flies at dusk. It's bland as junket....'

And she nods and smiles.

'It's reputation,' I go on. 'Reputation is a silk sack. Anything precious is found within. Possibly – an infinity of silk sacks. What fascinates is what is yet unsaid. What will Tuan, and those similar, do next? The person's been hoisted on a throne, a pinnacle: so – what's now? What's the plan? What's the secret, what's the flaw? What's the aim, or are there many – invasion, dictatorship, abdication?

'We made Tuan, we gave him more and more; like we applaud the artist to go higher and higher up the rope. Do we make the act? Or, surely, it's all been worked out and practised. Even if it's improvised – improvisation takes the most practise, best timing. We can't do any of that fancy stuff – our curiosity grows.'

She smiles and nods. I'm not in on this, I don't take rides with strangers. 'Let me off, Poirette,' I say. 'I'm not in this, this adventure that maybe no one knows exactly what it is, although it seems the means for anything at all, however large, have been prepared....'

'Help me with this stuff,' she says. 'I've more important things to do than file.'

'You're wrong,' I say, much irritated. 'The magician's me. I've made you all, I've drawn you. You are my true, my real – I've made you fuzzy, baggy, overblown and helpless.... I give you grunts and dialogue, you're an illusion caricatured.

'That army's just for boasting – it wouldn't serve, it wouldn't last. My big gun would take it out before reveille....

'I despair; as I drag you down, you're mute – you've no tale to tell, Poirette. Tuan's said it all, word for word, what he's just heard. He's the usurper of the familiar, he comes marching in brass boots, bearing a lily and a scimitar. And now he'll start to put his head on walls....'

It's true – once, he'd have put himself on stamps and coins, but now – he has to be a poster, an address on screens.

'What we see him do,' I say, 'Is of no interest. Not to him, or me ... maybe even not to you. It's of no interest compared with what he wants, and dreams he'll do. Perhaps he's planned the ultimate enormity he can, will do. Hang on! See where his bravado leads, see him spend fake notes, hand out free horse and coke, seduce, enrol....

'All that, repels me. It can be done, whatever scheme it is: it has been done, over and over, and it's grotesque. Monstrous.'

Poirette reacts at last. 'Umar, I don't know what you fear. You're on the list. We help you while we can. If you leave, your time here will weigh against you. You've picked up other brands and burns – you are a runaway, a maverick. You're wanted – but not by us!'

*

She's right. I fear the future, what will come, what's being prepared and what I cannot deal with, not having courage, determination. Who has those qualities? Do I speak for anyone but myself? Nothing fits, nothing is resolved, there's no direction – I can't give it one. But – Tuan: the lord of order. He has no prejudices, no preferences – so, he could espouse anything, any wish for death, his own, or anyone's at all. It's not Tuan's following of every platitude that terrifies – it's the belief that all will come out right – or will overcome, evade, disaster at the least, and leave him shining, safe and talking on – top of the pile of sinking lives....

Bland faith, banality, the calculated optimism, the cool hard head, the laugh that says 'all will be well'.... That's not the worst, they say: inaction and indifference, submission, hopelessness – that's the end: extinction. Tuan, his total dominance, is built on those, on that.

*

We're quizzed. 'frequent flyers' go in the front section of the plane. 'You've survived, and so the most dangerous place is yours' they say. 'give heart to all the rest.'

My neighbour laughs. '"Frequent flyers" – it used to be the mark of heresy – the Cathars were accused of night flying: bilocation, hosts of black angels ... the pact.'

'I know,' I say. 'Birds don't take aeroplanes. They scare too easily.'

'Is it a cure or a disease?' she asks. 'Flying from place to place?'

'I hope it's fleeing, with a hope of something absolutely new,' I say.

'Or absolutely old,' she adds. 'I feel it's like we're in a cart. One of those Romanian ones, with tall wheels; all of us clustered there, just like we've always been, the horses straining, slipping, falling, like the one the peasant killed in Dostoevsky. Raskolnikov's dream – it starts – "death will come and it will have your eyes". Your poetry, Umar, doesn't stick in the mind –

not at all. You stole! The wheels – a great invention – we can't go fast, but they master well the broken road. It's uncomfortable. But – we go on; we have, if not for always, for uncountable years, mutations – then something not accounted for occurs. The road. It ends. No one has thought this simple thought. There is no "on" to go.'

'Yes,' I say. 'We all think that. It's a banality. Just change the image, maybe it's a simile – and the road comes back. It's there ahead. A metaphor – nothing to fear.'

I try to soothe the panicked voice beside me, wishing she would find a twig of sanity and cling to it.

'Carpe diem,' she says, taking my hand and with the other opening a wicker bag, full of rolls of notes, vertical, sand-coloured, like classy wafers for ice creams: *gaufrettes*. 'This is for confusion,' she says. 'Look!' She selects a modest roll.

The notes say: 'Tequila dollars, issued in Chiapas: for the revolution.'

'I'm Dulcine,' she says.

They bring tequila – it starts to give lustre to the flight – all planes are painted black, the windows blacked out to calm our fear of heights and falls.

'Dulcine's a made-up name,' I say. 'Like Poirette.'

'They all are,' she says, 'Don't be picayune.'

We're very drunk. The plane lands – we can't see out. In flight, the crew has changed, they speak a language we don't understand. 'Do I get off here?' I ask Dulcine.

'Where were you going?' she asks.

The lavatory is a shack in a field of maize.

'I'll show the sights,' says Dulcine.

'Then, you know where we are, and it's where you, at least, were destined?' I say.

'I have the instinct, Umar,' she says. 'I recognise a sight. A bed, a bottle too. Cat, mouse, dog. You do all that at school.'

We're silly drunk. Dulcine books a room, the hotel staff gathers to laugh, makes fun of us, and shores us up. Her bag went forward with the plane. 'Oh, they'll bring it back,' she says, and we are satisfied they will.

'Now, Umar, you old bear,' she says, when we're alone, 'You mustn't hibernate. This is the time the two of us have sex with one another.'

And we do.

*

After a while, I say, 'This was not a good idea.'

'Umar,' says Dulcine, 'It wasn't an idea at all.'

For sure, that's true. 'Somehow,' she says, 'we fell into the world, with these bodies, that transmogrify. They have their seasons. They sleep, they run and leap, bodies we're not responsible for – their design, their speeds, deliberations, maladies – coloured in shades of black and grey, not our choice, of course.... We don't know why we're in them, we're not their authors, and we can't curate. Even if we try – we die. Instincts are still more incomprehensible – maybe they keep us upright and hungry, fearful and irascible.

'Now, what do you want, Umar? Not having done what's done? A watch that runs in reverse, so you can go back and have the identical time past again, but remembered better, more refined, perhaps?'

'You're right,' I say, 'I was ungenerous. And unrealistic too.'

*

The money is not returned. She says, 'It's all tequila dollars – I always fly on Mexican planes. As a frequent flyer, you should know.'

'Usually,' I say, 'I depend on people met quite casually, to offer work I didn't want.'

'We could do sponge fishing,' Dulcine says. 'If there's a sea. If not, most people without inspiration start a stall – fry little things. You could do it on a bicycle. Converted, naturally. Combine it with some simple crime. Find a policeman, cut them in, and they'll protect us, find us customers, and spring us out of jail.'

'It's fantasy, Dulcine,' I say.

'No no,' she says. 'That's what you do. It happens just as I am telling you. I know, trust me.'

She's right, and that is what we start to do.

*

It's not easy, and not what we want to do. But, if you are a pig, a sheep, a male animal, a chicken, say – life is quite short, and all's been set out and weighed. What we do is indeterminate, improbable. If things go bad, you're not killed, depilated, hung on a hook. There is no particular staging-post, no milestone, no tree you have to touch or well to throw a centime in.... No one takes care of you until they ship you to the abattoir. That's good, but you are not a cherished thing, you are too many, troublesome in everything you do.

'Death is the only thing I can give myself,' says Dulcine. 'But we're too busy. Sex – mostly I need someone else, and we can't afford booze, not with a label on the bottle, and what we do is inconclusive. It can go on for ever, you get to look old, very old, but maybe you are not. It doesn't prove a thing.'

'Some people do quite well,' I say. 'We don't know how to do it.'

'New ways of seeing?' Dulcine says. '*I* know. They'll make a movie of us, put it on TV.'

'I'm curious,' I say, 'But not an object of curiosity. When I've found a path, I'll say. Meanwhile....'

'Meanwhile, we've nothing,' Dulcine says. 'You're nothing, Umar. I set the pace – keep up, or quit the race.'

She makes it clear – the ad will go much better if it's her alone.

'People in our trade,' she says, 'Are informers, or they're militants. You're scared – you won't be either. Being on a list's enough for you to show that you resist. Really – you're a mystic. The unknowable attracts you, illusion is your bower and refuge. I know how to shift myself – you wait for lifts. You're plastic, packing – you seek out gaps, cracks, and fill them, jump right in....'

'Well, Dulcine,' I say. 'What's it to be – militants or narks? Which do you back?'

'You know I don't care,' she says, 'So long as I can travel, and have my sisters helping me, and them all free, of course.'

She's already in her movie. It's planned, ridiculous, all timed, located; the sequences, naturally – they're not sequential. I've no regrets, I leave her, the place, the bicycle, the much-worn frying oil – and join the smugglers delivering a string of donkeys, over the mountains, to another state. It's my scenario, improvised, but pegged to strings of time, lifting and imprisoned like laundry on a line.

State to state: Venezuela to Colombia, Lebanon to Syria, Turkey to Iran. We are always exiles, moving from exile to exile, never remembering, not having acquired a memory of time before, not remembering where we started; where we were before we are. We have to build ourselves, in storeys, like the totem dropping out the plane, or fortresses of logs prepared for winters in Siberia.

'You'll find someone, not a home,' Dulcine said. 'If you don't meet someone, stay at home and make some children.'

She sees it well – in life, there is no lasting drama – there are flashes of it, but they're mere hillocks and potholes.... Drama is the theatre: the gunshot. Opera is the catafalque....

Lives are racing circuits – take them fast or slow. There's the same finish-line for everyone.

My mate's Sahan. I ask to stay with them.

'*We* are a clan, Umar, he says. '*You* are a particle, without a substance. You can make up songs – they're not as good as those we know.'

'Don't be fooled,' I say. 'My name's a curse. I don't do poetry.'

'In the last resort,' Sahan says, 'You poets have in mind *l'amour*. Whatever else, whatever indignation, solitude, kinship with nature or the abstract – in a corner of your head there is a shrine. Love past, remembered, lost, regained.

'It's a lake of gasoline – stupid to put a match to it, but there it lies, iridescent, clogging lives and blackening greenery. Don't deny....'

'I yield to you, Sahan – poetry is not my thing,' I say. 'But Love has never been suggested.'

'We used to go for hostage-taking, Umar,' Sahan says, brisk at once. 'If things go bad again ... we'll start it up. If we need cash, it's no use asking somebody for it.

'You're on a list, Umar. Maybe you've been too strong on liberty or on coercion ... lilies or rockets: both at once? A communist, perhaps? The last, like that Japanese soldier on his desert island, fighting on alone, alone, against nobody at all? Discipline and freedom simultaneous?

'You're not in our game, you're not valuable to anyone. If you were an agent, spy ... you'd have a price....'

Given my work delivering cash, I maybe have a price, but not worth collecting it.

'The question,' Sahan says, 'Is not about the qualities, how to behave, feel gratified. We know all that. It's time. That is the problem: good times, bad times. If you want to make your own time, own space, you'll float. Times change – if you don't, you'll finish on a chain, in the stable. You have to face the stream – to reach another shore, you need to coax the current – it pushes you downstream, while you accept, insist. Insist, acccept – you make the crossing, but it's never straight across. Too stubborn – you will drown, or be a crazy nuisance, end shut, locked in....'

*

The boatman looks at us with disapproval, forgetting to dig in with his pole. We start to spin.

'It's taken hold,' says Julien, holding aloft his whisky bottle, offering me with gestures.... 'The whirlpool is within, I suffer it for you,' and he holds my shoulder, 'Not him –' pointing with disdain towards the poling matelot.

'No, no,' I say. 'I only take white spirits.' It's Dulcine's line.

'The spirit is colourless in all its forms,' he says, does not insist.

We climb up the bank; before us, a heathery plain. Juien has paid the perilous crossing, for the two of us.

'I'm finished for the day,' he says. 'Now, carry me. When you can blunder on no more, you'll see my caravan. Deposition. Lay me there. Anything you find – is yours. Take it, towards the fare, as you move on.'

All goes as he has said. I'm exhausted. He gathers strength next day – exercises, jumping up and down. 'Lungs, heart and liver. Things you'll never see, and take on faith that they are where they should be. They are one's obligations, sacraments: you must have faith. Mine – wavers. I have doubts. What if they don't exist? Your organs, rampaging in you, their cathedral? My doubts – harden into a suspicion.... Alas, my work – has quite enfeebled me....'

There's a folder. 'Ram', it says. *'catalogue raisonné'*. It's empty.

'The work is easy,' Julien says. 'You trace all Ram's creations, sculptures – through the world. The owners, shows, the prices. Print and publish. Most are *cire perdue*, they're multiples, but there are forgeries as well, many, a myriad ... replicas of replicas he's done, you'll need to spend some years in court, and you will lose, but then – there is the principle ... many pieces, all unsigned, and many arms, he was a devotee of Shakti, and his muse, Céline, works at a consulate – she'll explain.' He flags, says.... 'There's theories about art, and sex, abandon too – or thinking of it. Something else, giving up the inspiration, investing in a scheme. All those celebrities have a favourite – a war, disease, a bunch of mercenaries ... a cause. She will explain.'

Poor Julien. If you weren't yourself a drinker, he'd seem desperate and near the end. His is an excess of hedonism, nothing more....

'What's the deal?' I ask.

'The boredom of the task,' he says. 'Its fiddling, its nullity – can never be passed on – not wholly. Not to you, Umar. You are an amateur, a dropper-in. I seek a devotee. I have the type in mind, exactly.... I shan't forget my quest. We all must have one, evidently. But at least you earn the title – 'martyr to someone else's art.' You do the work, and I'll give you half of what I get from Ram.'

'That's more than generous,' I say. 'It's exactly what I want – nothing to steal, no crime, nothing emotional; no hooks and crooks ... No judgements, and no qualities. An artist – dead, or at arms length ... affirmed, trying to increase his worth ....many, many arms, a multi-skilling goddess .... Free to make things up ...'

'No, no! He'll be all over you. Ram's demanding,' Julien says. 'His lover, Céline, too. They fight each other for supremacy, but she'll get you the documents you'll need, the tickets and the intros.... You must recruit for him. His lawyers and his puffers too.'

*

'Again?' Céline asks. 'Another slave to inspiration? Not yours, not anyone's today – those statuettes, made for the spiritual, ages back. Instead – pop! Into commerce with them! Now, there's a charge of death and sex. Be careful, Omar. There's two types. 'Shakti one' – the power of women. Sex: Ram allows me four arms as a stimulus: he has six. On those statuettes, there are no attributes, no skulls: just fingers and a smile. Then 'Shakti two' – when we broke up, he made me a grotesque, bearer of death, with weapons to replace caresses. There's thousands – some are threats, some – promises of bliss. Catalogue each one, and he will go to law to seek his rights. No hope. There is no copyright on the divine.'

'I'm rather set aback, Céline,' I say.

She's a delight, but there's an angry streak. I see why Ram first adored her, then cast her as his fate.

Vinciane comes to my mind. 'This exoticism, sex and death,' Céline says. 'It's all a fraud. But he's traduced my image, made me a caricature. Help me get redress, find every copy, bring them to me – some are large, and some are gold, some are in bank vaults, some in the sea.... I'll reward you, Umar, make your fantasy come true....'

'Sex? Or death?' I ask, quite disturbed.

'Oh, silly boy,' says Céline, tweaking my nose. My, but she's strong.

'I can fly you, Umar, anywhere,' she says. 'It's our perk. Giving you a nationality: visas, to come and go. And see you through the customs, with your art, your toys, for Ram. Divinity. Me! If you don't return, wherever you're concealed – the consuls will deport you here. You'll be a parcel, tied with silk threads ... and I shall eat you for my five o'clock,' she says, mischievously. Her strength, her humour – not my thing at all. As for Shakti – I have always been, reluctantly, a faithful believer and practitioner of all her cults, except the wordy Californian ones.... Sex and death – they're all around: agnosticism isn't possible.

*

I complain to Julien. 'There's no protest. There's no class that can appropriate knowledge, let alone power. It's gone, or never was; or am I blind?

'You've worked, Umar – what did you learn?' he asks. 'Where were the proletarians? Gone under many sods. Nameless graves, a stratum of voiceless carapaces, worn out, a global mulch. Without the work of others, in a week we die, all of us – meanwhile, we avoid the toil, the effort: laborious labour. Power, giving orders – is so much more refined! History is overleapt – we return to origins, to instincts, the primal cave. All that has occurred, since the myth of our creation as subjects of invisible gods – all is forgotten, cast aside. Back we go. Monkey days. All struggle has been vain. We find our history on souvenir stalls, we gyre and flip between our fear of death, our hope that sex has some significance....'

'My work was disappointing, Julien,' I say. 'I won't bore you with the sex. It's been irrelevant. No meaning, or a puzzle....'

'Oh, it has meaning,' says Julien, pouring us stiff tots. 'Sex means that death's not final. Life rises from the grave. Procreation gives the lie to our extinction – on and on it goes, till death is the consolation for no more sex. If you found it all so great, that is,' and he laughs.

I think of Vinciane. 'Desire is fun,' I say. 'But after climax what is next? What's left?'

'Death': says Julien, happy that his equation has been demonstrated. 'Sculpture, for a few. Mostly, we have one idea, and spend our lives trying to make it clear. An acronym, an epitaph. Of course, Ram's idea has no legs. He might want to put together sex and death – but that was established at the start. He began with that, it's a given. Shakti already embodies both. He separated them. They are inseperable forever, my poetic friend! He's understood at last – and now he goes to court, and probably to war, to turn his inspiration into cash.'

'Céline thinks he has no hope,' I say, much depressed.

'Paints and mistresses,' Julien says, 'That's why artists want the cash. But Ram is past the sex, and there's mechanical reproduction of his toys... It's reputation that he wants. You don't get that from law.'

*

'Julien was a fighter,' Céline says. 'So strong, he was the only one able to control himself. He broke himself with booze, pretended he would work for Ram. He's a martyr. Ram's a warrior. You'll see – no one breaks him. As for you, Umar, you're a feather. Cause trouble, and I'll blow you up and blow you down.'

'Strong talk, Céline,' I say. 'It's the task. I shan't do it, because I can't. It's impossible. Moreover, if I were to try, it wouldn't be worthwhile. The only point is Ram – and I don't care. He's nothing to me, I am not his slave.'

'You hoped to be,' Céline says, 'Until the work became too hard.'

*

'It's trivial,' says Julien. 'The work they hoped I'd do: was that the best I might have done? And so – perhaps it was.'

When Ram comes he's not impressive as a presence – but his reputation makes him large. He says, 'I'm sure you've been informed. Julien is broken, you're a lightweight, Umar, but you do what you are told – or even what you think might be implied. Céline's abandoned, so she becomes grotesque, but she controls the flights.... I have a force – platoons of lawyers, fighting for me. When I win my case, I'll have the cash....'

'To pay the lawyers, Ram,' I say. 'Don't take me for a patsy. Won't do and can't do – they're very close, and that's an edgy couple – won't do's resistance, can't do's surrender....

'Your inspiration, Ram, the story you are in – it's tightly worked, the theme is large, if cloudy, overwrought and over-worked. Is it worthwhile? The biggest themes are the most trite. This searching for the origins, ur-women, ur-warriors, all that – it's your idea, I'm sure....'

'Mostly we all have one idea,' he says. 'Though mostly, we have none. It should occur to you, Umar, whose namesake fished out every image and soft perception we all know from infancy, that in the end that one idea ... is all the same. There's one idea. The big one, Umar. And it's mine. I let you think it is your own, and I am still the beneficiary. *My* ancestor slew monsters – many more, more thoroughly, than Siegfried: communed with nature, made allies human and inhuman too, fought battles, escaped ambuscades – flew, swam, and trekked....'

'We all do that, Ram, frequently,' I say. Frequent Flyers come to mind. 'Doing your will may cost. To show your confidence, a something on account would help....'

The conversation stalls. Ram says if I can't catalogue his work, he'll have it all collected, sent here, and auctioned.

'It would be too drastic,' Céline says. 'Dramatic too. It's too difficult for us. We're empty barrels. Julien – he'll go abstemious, thin and sallow, die sober, and for what? Umar we know about. And me – they'll send me to Kabul – a provocation. My bosses specialise in that, it's good, except they stay back home. In the consulate, I'll be a bright loquacious bird among those poor peahens, harassed and silent. So much for powerful women, Ram. Your tribute looks precious and antique, when you let in a glim of realism....'

'Reality, you mean,' says Ram. 'If I had all my work to hand, in the mass – maybe it would seem complete. I'd close it somewhere, move on. Having it scattered, traded, travestied and copied, shut in books, museums ... it's taxidermy. Get rid ofit! And I could be a hero for quite another cause....'

'The only cause,' Céline says, 'You've ever countenanced, is yours.'

'Since I went to law,' says Ram, ignoring her, 'I'm drawn to it. Not to my case, or cases. It's the power. Its autonomy, the ceremonial – especially the power no dictator, no president could ever have. To send you to a jail, and keep you there, to death row, or to some long execution – disease, or madness, judicial killing, deportation, solitary. The international court, tribunals, courts martial and commercial – sentenced to bankruptcy and suicide ... for a word, a sentence, a prompt; a document not shown or slipped clandestine into someone's dossier. And lists. You won't get off the list, even if you're millions, more than a continent, all guilty, no appeal. Every action – is it legal? Or more likely, not. Terrorism's nothing, when terror's all around.

'The power, Umar! You recognise it when a feather from it brushes you, falls in your drink ... and you are fleeing, being trapped! You're a prisoner, anonymous, under the gun. 'strip off, open your hidey-hole, your arse, your last safe place, your strongbox' ... then, comes the prison mouse, morse on the water pipes....'

'Everybody knows this,' says Céline. 'When it suits, people protest. And more laws come....'

'You haven't understood,' says Ram. 'The law is air. We breathe it all the time. But it's dispersed. Breathe in – expel. The power of the law, if it were concentrated...! The lawyers – those samurai – they need a code of honour. And an employer, a big boss.

'What price the hits and misses of the arts, the higgledy-piggledy interventions of the spirits, malign, benign, asleep, beseeched, blasphemed...? Chaos, ephemera....

'If it were concentrated, all that power.... Autocrats must think before they act, they risk comeuppances, revolts. They're flighty, unpredictable ... They have soft spots. But law! – it hits us all the time. An insult to a judge – you disappear – "take him down": that is his phrase.'

'Don't forget, Ram,' I say, getting bored, exasperated. 'Give something on account, to start me off.'

*

'You want dictatorship for ever, harder, harsher, Ram,' says Julien. 'You'll fail, but to bring you down – there'll be a terrible collapse, and massacres – the hecatombs! The pyres, the human flesh, burning – reaching the clouds where gods sit, nostrils ready for the tribute – smoke, Ram, all smoke!'

'I'll change my name,' says Ram. 'It's too intrusive. I'll change, utterly, and use my soft approach.... It's done everywhere, with faith or principles, tradition spruced, or modernity refined. I bring the science, the doped bonbons. The compendium. All human behaviour ... defined and catalogued. Deviance punished without appeal....'

He wears some classy running shoes – he scampers off, bouncing off walls, doing a curlicue, a ballet step, challenges the skateboarders to a pirouette.

'Art's a disease,' Céline says, 'but you can cure yourself. Mastering the world – it doesn't always follow art, usually artists are too old and poor, the unheard, the unsold.... But Ram is vigorous and rich.'

*

Later, I tell Céline. 'I'm on the list. So, I can't fly – I would be caught, Céline.... Don't clear me, please don't book me....'

'Don't tell me that,' she says. 'And don't appeal to my good side – I scraped it off against a tree.'

'It's so I can't work for Ram,' I say. 'It is the law. I'd land in jail.'

'If I don't accredit you to leave, you would stay here,' she says.

'No, I promise,' I say. 'I'll be gone. It's my turn for a lucky episode, a lucky strike, they say.'

'They might strike oil in your armpit,' says Céline. 'Otherwise, you're dross.'

'It wouldn't be luck, if it happened,' I say. 'Chance, maybe; but welcome. My problem is, that things don't fit. No one but me can toss a coin that never comes down heads. No one seeks their qualities – and finds they don't exist.'

'Well,' says Céline. 'You're special, unique. Better than being lucky. Everybody's lucky, once in a while: you never are. Someone in the sky has it in for you. You're special for them.'

She smiles at me. I'm filled with dread. Suppose she takes a shine to me.... I say, 'Does Ram have contacts? Can he spread his big idea?'

'Ram says an artist has nothing that inheres – not gender, colour, politics – that stuff,' she says. 'It's all afflatus, inspiration that descends – a gift. There's nothing inside the creator – it all begins and ends outside. Is there some origin in Ram? Bihar or Bahia? Who cares? Do you? He has no origin: he's all reception. The voice speaks through him – he's a shell, a tube, a horn.'

I don't challenge, don't explore. I hope the subject can move on....

'I'm fascinated by the lives of people relatively poor; dropping in on them, when I was a spy – Ossetia, Libya: their hospitality, intelligence – and always a war, terrible, to come, or past....' I say. 'I suffer for them – uselessly. My eye, Céline, it has a cast, it sees through time; its spyglass – is the hole in the seer's small secret stone.... For sure, you don't understand me....

'I fear Ram has gone it wrong. Not a simple cult of death – we lived through that. The spirit came to earth and picked us off, everything got worse. Shakti; sex and death, instead. If we felt like either of them, it would cohere, would work: hedonism and sobriety. It suits. It's personal, and nihilistic. An autocrat will come – to make the rules, or to relax them....'

'Ram has ambitions,' Céline says, seeming to pay no heed. 'Wars don't come into them. The tall poppies among states have managed recently not to go to suicidal war, head on with one another. Now, those wars exported, once fought by proxy and far off, are rather close ... refugees you can confine in tents, but in the end....' She stops, and gestures.

'Go on, Céline,' I say.

'In the end ... we contemplate an end. Or even – stasis. Like before new empires start,' she says, 'or there's a hatch of them, like frogs. It's irresolute. Unresolving. You, I – need a bedfellow you can hug....' She ogles me. It's frightening. Sex or death – neither attracts.

'You could dry out Julien,' I say. 'Reformed alcoholics – they're very orderly. Pal with him. He's visited death from both sides – nothing is concealed.'

'He waxes his moustache, I'm sure,' she says, dismissing him. She's a dilemma.

'Prejudice, Céline,' I say. 'Racism, sex, nation and descent. It's not ideas, not analysis, that count. Our future lies in ignorance, error, and stupidity. Ram stands aside from that, he cultivates his own silliness and ignorance and mistakes.

'In the world, it won't be sex and death that dominate – it's sex "with who?" "Death at whose hand?"'

She doesn't follow me. 'It's countries and rules, Umar,' she says. 'Borders and orders. Believe me. I'm paid to know.'

'It's not what I want,' I say.

'You should set easier questions,' she says.

'It's not the answers that's difficult,' I say, 'It's the people.'

'Then you'll have to invent the ones you like,' she says.

That's the end of the beginning and end of our intimacy.

You can't try out people like horses. If they let you, even in those huge markets on the steppe ... you probably have to judge by look, not trot. If you can't do that, no one would sell to you. It's very difficult.

Céline's a biter, you can see. Anyway, I don't want a friend, I need an ally.

*

The doctor says to Julien, 'I think you came to me too late. I see in your fear-filled eye – a design. Homicide or suicide. You're not the murdering type – maybe, of yourself, but there it ends. You must accept – when death comes, it is because he finds his time, the gap – your foil is high, that's good. But death is tall. His weapon comes down, over your guard, straight to your heart. He is a sporting type – you could attack. But no one does. You shake; your reactions – almost zero. Defence is the worst form of self-protection, but alas, it is the only one...

'When he comes, it is the time. Relax. Enjoy what's left of hours and days. You life is full – or rather, Julien, you've been full most of your life, topped up. The booze – it gives you pleasure and much pain, but protects you from the pleasure and much pain you'd face if you'd been lucid, sober all the time. In the end, the account is just the same – you will not owe a cent. All is paid off.... You exit penniless but free.... The last few obols, if you have some left, will just about be my fee.

'But, a doubt remains....'

'Why?' asks Julien, 'Why must I face death with my weapon, useless, and no mask? My owner, my employer Ram – he determined so. My task for him was monstrous....'

'No,' says the medic, 'It's not so. Employers don't have that right ... the most they do is fire you, and you're free.'

Julien flickers out, a candle in a draught. No hope – the life announced the death. The catalogue raisonné, Shakti, the degradation and the falsity of Céline ... impossible and unavailing to tell a doctor all that *fanfaronnade*. A doctor sets you up for death, teaches the fencer's basic moves – the feet skewed, uncomfortable; the target – you – dressed up in white. You're not allowed a mask. A single hit, a touch ... you're pinked ... stiffed ... skewered.

It's a set-up, no contest: your resistance – vain.

That was you done, Julien. Nothing to do with Ram, his untold wealth, family connections, inflated desires ... each time you switched on something – up came his logo, and he made a buck. On that basis he proposed to rule the world – like all the other rich guys, warlords, presidents of this and that.

'All nonsense,' says Céline. 'Julien – you're dying early because of drink. You've made your organs small, rubbery, and black. Like balls for fives or squash. Forget the fencing talk – you've done it to yourself, my dear. And handed on to Umar everything you didn't want to do, and left him trying to get out of it.... So much for you, Julien, and your moustache....'

Céline would be the next to go.

'There's no conspiracy, Umar,' she says. 'I'm tragic. I'm abandoned, gnarled with despair, neglect.... A nobody. I've no wish to end like Julien, I live clean and poor. The boss finances every cause – humanist, occult ... his money runs – floods of dry water, permeates all lands.... For me, a drought; I'm parched. I'm small fry, Umar. No one looks for me, or does me down....'

It's true: we two are too small to crush.

All that money produces monsters, some elected. Ram's at home with monsters, indifferent to us.

Céline takes my arm. With Vinciane – a tragedy. With Céline, I fear – catastrophe.

'Where are we going, Céline?' I ask.

'Nowhere,' she says. 'Home.'

'That's what I feared,' I say. 'Nowhere's the place I don't want to be.'

'You don't have much choice,' she says. 'It's the best deal open.'

I'm no longer responsible for the world, I think. No one is, no one has been. But – at least, negotiate for myself? It's folly, even to consider it. I do. I should consider Céline as well. I do.

'Don't wait, Céline,' I say. 'I remember something.'

I remember not to forget.

'We closed his grave,' Céline says. 'You've all your life left to remember things.'

I sidle off. Don't say 'farewell' – it starts the saga off again. Keep quiet. Just depart.

She'll be next to go. She's seen how it's done.

*

'You worked for Ram. For Shakti, I should say,' a little guy called Prospero intercepts me, shouts out, as I canter off. He works in the bottling plant nearby – a smell of beets and apricots around him – some stay in their sugar, others ferment....

'All of us can choose a cult,' he says. 'They said philosophy was dead. A cult, though, you can believe ... not its cosmology, of course, but the senses, colours, combattents.... It will protect, as well as any other tale. You meet good guys. The parties – they're wilder than a club, there's no time or other limit. You go on till you have had enough....'

'The stories, Prospero,' I prompt. 'They must inspire.'

'You follow them,' he says. 'You tire. Then find another series. It's not TV – you're actively involved.'

'Do you believe?' I ask, 'The themes? Or that divinities can intervene with you and me....'

'The theme is sex and death – we all believe in that,' he says. 'As for the meddling of the gods – if you have tossed a coin, you know there's luck involved – like at the races, and with numbers of all kinds. You call it luck when yours comes up – all you need believe is that there is luck, not chance, involved. Luck is an intervention – chance means we're alone, that anything at all can happen, no warning, and no defence. No one to mourn....'

'Ram has moved on....' I start. 'To autocracy by law....'

'Who cares?' asks Prospero. 'The cults, the heresies, abound, there is no common core to them except for death and sex – all the rest is "all the rest". We suffer now from law and crime, but in the end our creed is pure and true....'

He pauses, I remember Céline.... I wonder if she's in a cult, or maybe she's become one – adored, invoked, and even bilocating when there's a party and a wake....

'Go on,' I say. 'They say the end is nigh unless there is some luck, some action, sacrifice and suffering....'

'Exactly so,' he says. 'If there's an end, nothing I do will work. Besides, they say each of us comes to an end, so what we do is better done in colour, with a shout, than hiding underneath the sheets and reading Proust.'

'You seem a thoughtful type,' I say. 'We could exchange some thoughts, and even, if there is a ceremony, induction, ecstasy, or just a smoke and drink with some good guys – you could accompany me, and after, let me rest....'

'Rest's a slice of time,' he says. 'But really – time can't be sliced. Cash will come into it, my friend. Payment's always in the real; real time. But still, time doesn't measure reality, you see. What's real is the passing image that appears between "gone past" and "future inexistent yet to come". Reality is the frame in a movie except you're in it, while you're watching it. The real is real, of course – it's where your luck comes in, if it is due. If not – bad luck! The rest is speculation, except for sex and death. No sex, there's no one left. No death – there's everyone! A crowd of hasbeens, living ghosts. The cult....'

'I see,' I say. 'The cult is luck! It's like a rabbit's foot, a spit, a blowing on the dice....'

'Of course,' says Prospero. 'And fun is fun – and absolutely real. Drink and sex – avoiding death – what more do you expect?'

'Avoiding?' I ask. 'There's no avoiding anything.'

'It's where your luck, divinity, comes in,' he says. 'Just suppose – the guys decide to have a human sacrifice – your luck lies in not being it! Of course, it isn't usual – but it's real.... If you're lucky, you have sex – might we say the same of death...? Lucky to have it, lucky not. It's inescapable, so there must be luck for when it comes, or not.'

'I get your drift,' I say. 'I just request – not luck, but recuperation on your floor, divan; a mattress ... anything. No luck's involved, I'm sure.'

He's unenthused. Orgiastic cults should open people up, make them more generous.... He's not into that, a sharing round.

I say, 'I'm sure, even without Ram, these cults will sweep the world – Americans already nearly there, the Russians always were. China will hold out, I'm sure....'

'I'm not bothered,' Prospero says. 'It's not about recruiting. Ram just caught a trend. It's all the same to me if I'm alone, or in a tiny sect. In fact, it's better so, better alone and right than having millions, in error and excess, all following a muddy path that leads to hell. What matters is the truth, and that I have.'

'It seems to me,' I say, 'you're a Jensenist, my friend. On the edge: a rocky ledge. Take your pleasure quietly, anathema to misbelieve ... and wait for death and hope your judgement will be quick and clement.

'There's others – bully boys – exaggerate.... They'll beat you down and blow you up. There will be conflicts between cults – not that anyone believes there's anything beneath, a depth. It will be behaviours, misbehaviours, that cause the wars, the schisms....'

'And interests too,' he says. 'And as for you, Umar, for me, poetry's superfluous. But since you plead: one night. Just one. Then, out you go. No bringing in heretical mates. No lounging, singing, making rhymes. No booze that's not been blessed.'

He is not generous. All night, he strums and plucks – a one-stringed fiddle? A lute? Prayer?

Ineffable: more would be too much.

'I'm sure you had no rest,' he says. 'It was my music. I'd have liked to sleep, but you were there. I impressed you, I am sure.... You can't have too much spirituality, don't you think?'

'Oh,' I say, 'I was wondering about the bottles, that was all. Bottling, bottling – all day, for ever … empties welcomed, then fill, fill, fill. Plenitude – but not consumed. Not, at least, by you … Sleepless, you might mistake your roots for shoots....'

'I might indeed,' he says, with some bravado. 'I often do. But, the point is this. Listen! The ancients – they glimpsed the self-absorption of the divine, of what they called the gods. Self-contemplation was the sole concern of all the spirits – the meaning, purpose of the "this", the "that" – the everything. Nothing more, or "deep", or what we call the "spiritual". Ah! the indifference, the play, the sport they had with us, we fragile hopeful beings! How the spirits love processions, dances, killing animals and sacrifices – real know-nothings!

'And of course the humans copy, mirror, this ineffable self-absorption. Who, after all, invented who? Did we create the gods, their heavens, or was it them invented us?

'We want to steal a march on everyone, but still be civil, smooth: be loved, be rich, be lucky. We aspire to that, it is the human destiny, our condition. It's self-defence, self-love, but we present it as a striving for perfection, success in developing our loftier selves.... Humanity! Our vaunted potential, our being special, clever, self-improving, is really our indifference to the rest; our self-absorption. It's our characteristic, like the skunk's spray, the rattler's rattle.

'The trick is this: in recognising heavenly self-absorption – we can overlook our own.... It's how we get to be one up....' He looks hard at me, in triumph. 'That's how we recognise our fate,

and the indifference, the nullity, of any higher purpose. So –
what's left?'

'Not much,' I say, not following; my mind full of crushed
turnips and cauliflowers, fermenting ... in the huge shiny stills....

'We can get lucky!' he says, triumphantly. 'When you know
everything – try your luck. That is what is left!'

'I guess that's what the Chinese learned from the Tibetans,' I
say, quite at a loss. 'Maybe that's what the Han hoped to acquire
when they came and settled in.'

'You're fantasising,' he says sharply, 'How does that relate?'

'Nothing,' I say. 'Forget religion, forget the Buddha. Just –
where does luck come from? Where's it been, for ever; dropping
on us, like....?'

'Who knows?' he says. 'Who cares? Perhaps, if you're lucky,
you'll find out. If not – what difference does it make? The point
is that knowing won't make it drop on you!'

That's true. At least, Prospero has made it true, for everyone.
While I reflect on this, I start to understand Vinciane – the
mystery of what our casual encounter meant. What did she want,
what tie, what relationship? If what remains is luck – what
obligations hold?

'Honour, duty'? Surely not. But perhaps a moral sentiment,
that lingers.... Chimps have it, so humans may as well. Gratitude,
reciprocity, collaboration. These remain, if only for a while,
when there has been an interaction, some mutual task, a
gratification. Sharing establishes a mutuality, a recognition of
another's worth, or even their equality. There's been a
collaboration with a mate, a comrade, that will sustain a link.
Even if the association fails ... you've done it, both of you!

I say to Prospero – 'Monkeys who help each other climb a banana tree – they don't rely on luck, or hope for it. It's being monkeys ... makes a bond.

'There is no place at all for luck in that. I think what you wait for – luck – is what's left over when there's nothing more, no interaction, nothing shared, no sociality....'

'No,' he says. 'Luck's what makes sociality worthwhile and possible. It may be all that's left – but left it is, and sticks.'

*

I don't ask him for another night of rest – he's told me 'no', and now the monkey talk has made me feel quite unprepared to argue and discuss. I seem a romantic, a sentimentalist. Quite infantile and insubstantial.

'Neither of us knows enough to argue their complicated case,' I say.

'I'm more intelligent and worldly wise than you,' he says, 'But I agree.'

'Wise?' I ask.

'I own this little house – more of a hut,' he says. 'Thanks to the bottling plant. Everything's preserved, most goes to alcohol....'

'Maybe you'd put in a word for me?' I ask. 'Work, possibly?'

'I'll have to ask an agent's fee,' he says. 'I'm not an agent, naturally, so it will mean you paying in advance.'

It isn't what I want – or need. I'll go back to origins ... be a hunter ... draw on walls.

*

We long for hope, it doesn't come. It seems it should arise from us, within. There is no other referent but us. It means we hope for hope, and have to make it fruit – if we know how.

Prospero, his nasty creed, orgies that don't stimulate, the waiting for a lucky break – it's nihilism. Julien – sunk by his own intake, the bottling plant his resource and his comeuppance ... Céline, a victim of Ram's wealth and skittishness ... clutching at straws like me...

I take stock: money, sex, death, ghosts – a thriller, a weepie, politics, the supernatural. Start anywhere with those, continue, ignore, exploit, the genres: and that's my story. No end to any of the exploits, and vengeance, squads of it, is bound to come. I pretend I've done good in life, at least have tried, at least I have it on my list.

I'm on a list – that should be enough.

Some places, it's a pleasure to be poor – others, you suffer, you're counted, and have to hide yourself.

*

'... and the brown horse wins!' The loudspeaker! – very loud ... all laugh, we're thousands, betting on the blacks and greys, no one chose the brown ones, taking the places too. We're all cheerful, losers together, leaving the track. I'm absolved – I took my stake from Propero's stash, a tiny tax, now lost, and so I'm clean. This is the story of my world, my story of the world.

*

So, on and on. Prospero no more, and as in every story, you move through the cast until the music stops. There's one chair left, for you: maybe a divan, a *chaise longue* for two.

'Where I live now,' I say, 'many die young, really young. The rest live till they're very very old. It's because it's fruitful for philosophy. When you're ancient, there's not much more you can do. You think: discover secrets, or that there's none, and either way don't pass the insight on.

'My friend – she died very young before she could be diagnosed, so its hard for me to make a lesson from her. Songs of the death of children – make them beautiful, there's nothing more to do. I'm not sure I want another adventure. They don't live up to what they seem.'

'You're living wrong,' Malek says. 'Your attitude to work – it doesn't bring you closer to the poor – it only makes *you* poor. Work. You're an inconstant bore. Work as an intellectual....'

'There's none left,' I say. 'Not in advanced places....'

He goes on, 'You must help make the state, not rant about a personal world where you are free and leisured.... Only the right state can let you do exactly what you know is needed....'

'It's from despair,' I say. 'My doubts come from what has always been. Despair well grounded in defeats gone by and cataclysms yet to come....'

Malek and Ariane have found me, sit with me, and talk up what they're trying to do. You need a lot of cash for what they plan, not only manifs and some preacher men ... but, all cash is poisoned – in your pants it festers, turns your body lizard green.... I still deliver, sometimes: as an agent, a ganster, not a thief....

'I've been betrayed,' I say. 'Almost always. Part of a much greater treason ... greed and inefficiency....'

'Yes,' says Ariane. 'You must forget your anarchism, your littleness. You must make the state, make progress, be progressive: join the rest of those like you. What you have now is fusty, fantasy. Bring everybody in, you'll find there's lots like you and I who're *sympatique*.'

'Construct,' says Malek. 'There is always that, even if it's only speculation. Others will gather round, you'll be pioneers. You won't kill the people you find there, you'll teach them to use stirrups, make the horses run on faster, and you won't fall off so much.'

'Make the statesmen vegans,' says Ariane. They look at me, proud they've made me better. I wish it worked like that. 'Make defences so strong they can't be overthrown,' she says.

'I'm too frivolous to be an intellectual,' I say. 'I'm a butterfly – Amazonian, a metre wide from tip to tip, moon-yellow, fragrant – if they're not all extinct.'

'We were there,' says Malek. 'Last year, the big fry-up. No, no butterflies. And the people – even if you want to save them – they know better! Who'd trust you?' And we laugh.

'I know the case for a strong state,' I say. 'Everyone defending it against – what? Who can tell? Reactionaries, cash, more countries, more and more....

'Money and the powers corrupt ... I'd resist, of course, but there might be a limit ... my flesh is strong, but unreliable. It's been too often corrupted, and decomposed....'

'We might go together somewhere you've not been,' says Malek, 'Somewhere we know, that is entirely different.'

'Suppose,' I say, 'The world is like a super Roman Empire. Capitals all over, Rome, Byzance, Ravenna, Berlin, Beijing and San Francisco. With governors, rival emperors, and legionaires –

barbarians of all stripes, and Romans too, a few; who might they have been? ... Trojans coming from the sea, perhaps, becoming Greek and Croatian, Rumanian and African; worshipping the Northern and the Eastern gods, worshipping themselves, high priests of the cult of self, falling in love with Amazons, Egyptians, importing dogs from Trebizond....'

'Why bring in the dogs?' asks Ariane. 'You were doing fine – except the Romans overstretched, becoming something quite another. Too bad, the strife, the vanity.... If your orange is the world, that's it! It's round and sweet, it can't get bigger than it is.'

'You're not with me, Ariane,' I say. 'It's the system: the world, what ties it all together. Pith and rind ... the pips.... It's not about the oranges – it's that the oranges grow on trees! The culture, the cash, the competition – sport, games, the protocols, the treaties and the spats, the calibres are standardised.... Beggars and generals, ATMs that dispense ecstasy, scissored flowers by air and goats for Eid. Defended by a Wall, by severed heads, by passport control.... It's not a globe – it's nets in nets ... branches, branch plants, roots and trunks....'

Nature, fermented in the bottling plant.

'That's how it looks from your space, Umar,' Malek says. 'It's not like that close up.'

I think of Carthage, impregnable from the sea, but encircled, taken by land, destroyed to ankle-height, and sown with salt.... Palmyra, collapsing when the water disappeared, its merchants with an entrepot in Kerala.... Manichaeans nearly making it – another universal creed, one that would suit us better than the prissy monoliths, where you could take a side that had a chance against the tyranny of 'good'....

'And every week – Vesuvius! Who will be gawping at us when we're excavated...?'

'Don't be too much an intellectual,' Ariane says. 'You'll never leave the ground like that.'

'We'd like to see these messy places be like France,' says Malek, 'But without the history, and without the French.'

'In a way, Umar,' says Ariane, 'It's true. There are more centres, more peoples want to enter, modify, bring in their ideas and customs – and the space diminishes; armies proliferate, all want to make a little empire, a fortress for security, for valour, for vainglory, profit and survival.... That's why we need the law for all: and uniformity – no one big enough to dominate, no one so small it risks absorption....'

'I've worked for powerful people, Ariane,' I say. 'Myself – I haven't changed. If you've electors, if you've cash – you can change your mind, have people re-interpret your ideas ... It's a different scene....'

'Yes,' Malek says. 'Forget your exploitation and your sentimental jousts. You know Saodat, you know Ram. Protection of small states, the standard law, powerful and obeyed. And, you're still a spy, a courier – it makes you an asset, quite unparallelled....'

I reflect. It could be true. Except, to me, my life is Vinciane, Céline; where I could be an actor, show my qualities. Bond.

*

'You and Malek,' I ask her. 'Am I to think you're intellectuals? If so, I could dispute with you....'

'You said it yourself, Umar,' says Ariane. 'There's no intellectuals. Don't you remember? There was a *trahison des clercs*, then there was the urgency to climb aboard the trucks beflagged, and mix in with bearded revolutionaries, or the smooth devil-worshippers aboard.... Marx said it; that the intellectuals had done their job – they'd brought understanding of the world, as there still is. We know exactly what is to be done, usually can't do it....

'Philosophy is skinny, and impoverished. Now, you need people who would change the scene. The enlightened ones, their reason and their tolerance, were limited. Maybe reason works with science, not with our species. Hit and miss, trial and error – work better than reason anyway, more concretely. Tolerance will get you stasis, leaving things exactly as they are.'

'It could be, Umar,' Malek says, 'That you are indeed an intellectual – thinking, not doing, but with no career, no reading list, no publications, no appearances, no claque....'

'If I am,' I say, 'It doesn't seem a worthy thing to be.'

'That's up to you, and no one else, to say,' says Ariane. 'But – you have contacts that are valuable. You strike the big cheeses as disinterested: a strange one, not liking effort, but taking only small amounts of cash.'

'I heard this all before,' I say. 'It doesn't give me lustre, but it doesn't signify you're right. Who cares if there aren't intellectuals? Besides, it's an introduction that you want, you're not seeking critics, nor analysis.'

I could say 'No: I won't be an intermediary.' It isn't much. It would make trouble, though.

In the end, they use my name, discard me. Ram and Saodat remember me – they're interested in what Malek and Ariane want. It could gratify them all, be profitable.

I think – Malek's an *intelligent* – not an intellectual. I'm probably *intelligentskii* ... a dilettante, wordy faker ... educated to follow orders.

But there's the trap I dug, and fell right into it.... The chatter about intellectuals was vapid. It's clear, Malek and Ariane aren't theorists – they're conveying borrowed cash and wanting a commission ... wanting someone to carry the brown bag, the loot.

But, my self-absorption had me blunder on....

'It's weird, but not unusual,' says Ariane. 'That so much has gone on over your head, or so much ordinary banality lay beneath your field of vision. For us, the large accomplishments mean taking risks – that, they should have taught at school. Improving people's lot is hard. They resist as if they don't want it; and getting the capital together is an enterprise!'

'I think I knew that Ram was unpredictable and Saodat was bent,' I say, sarcastically. 'I can see that you're the good guys, Malek and you. I never have a project, so I can't dissent.... You've found a country – parts are up for sale. You take the risk, the benefits – the satisfaction too. All changes – some win, most don't. This place is tighter tied into the world, its system.... The consequences....'

'Are unpredictable,' says Ariane, 'Whatever you suppose.'

We leave it there.

*

They take me – the simpleton – along, to see how it turns out.

'They have a vote here,' Malek says. 'But rarely votes decide what we bring in.'

'You're in an opera-house, the theatre,' says Ariane, 'You don't use votes to change the plot, and who survives.'

'It's so,' I say. 'Even if you're in the opera, it's hard to change the music as you trek along. A route march on your diaphragm.'

Buying and selling, there's no need to hide, but Malek and Ariane aren't acting for themselves, but it's clear someone else is backing them. Real people, or, like Shakti, super-real.

They don't have money. They're a stalking horse, false competition, a fake offer to drive up other proposals, make everyone look shady, perhaps. Mediators. Sorting hostages, paying groups to do or not to do. Just prospecting – in the soil, in heads.

Outside – there's the Sahel. I can't leave the hotel room. There's metal shutters – light comes, but mostly goes.

The food looks like it comes off an aeroplane. We have the whole floor for ourselves – I can't get off it. 'It's too bad,' says Ariane, 'It's the security. We're meeting people in your room.'

'Give us a conspectus, Umar, if you can,' says Malek. 'Even something lyrical, if you must....'

'I'm just a spectator, seeing nothing,' I tell them. 'I imagined camels, Dogons, museums in the sand. Touaregs....'

'All that, you see on the TV,' says Ariane. 'It's on continually. Don't mention Touaregs, though. Or farmers, herders, people in the north. Don't talk of religion, dealing, armies, massacres. The colonial powers – they're like the Han. They don't appreciate nomads, even if they've settled down. Everything has changed – the desert, trade, the armies and the states.... Everything above ground is being carted off – what's underground awaits....'

'I'd guessed,' I say, 'Prospecting rights! That's why you're here. Potentially....'

'Yes,' Malek says, 'Potentially a fortune – dig it out, if it is there....'

'They don't let the sun in to these rooms,' I say, 'It's like we are denatured, underground: blind miners. The camels read the unmarked tracks, but us – we're lost.'

'See no evil,' Malek says. 'That's best. Don't speak, there's no one listening – and don't trust what you see, or hear.'

'I love the Sahel, Malek,' I say. 'I have my analysis ... Bury me in Ouadâne...'

'We won't be staying long enough to hear you out,' says Ariane. 'Remember – it's security. Everything's as it is for reasons of security. You're always the sentimentalist, the moralist – don't try to pin responsibilities.... If you like, everyone's to blame, and no one too. The space, the distances, the light, the colours of the skins, the resonance of the ambitions, the illusions ... an immensity burning out, destroying, easily destroyed....'

'I can't stand being shut in,' I say. 'Soldiers....'

'There's camels on TV,' says Malek, 'Like Ariane says. When there's electricity.'

And there he leaves it.

*

'The rules are very complicated,' says Ariane, when we land, back where we were. 'So intricate, so many actors. It's as if there are none ... no rules, and then no actors.'

'Or they're broken,' I say. 'The desert says you don't kill co-religionists, a Muslim doesn't kill another Muslim. It clearly isn't so.'

I remember – 'honour and duty' – that's one of the rules for rulers. For someone met on a train, they don't apply. I shall never be a ruler, and I'm glad. A ruler might try to be honourable, ordinary people can't.

'We two go through the controls so easily,' says Malek, angry and frustrated – 'And you, Umar, take hours. What's the secret?'

'No secret,' I say, 'It's the list. And going to the desert makes me more suspect.'

'You can't play muddy games without a team,' says Ariane. 'You'll be our prop.'

'Being detached,' says Malek, 'Gives you authority. If you tried, exerted, we'd see you're not quite up to it.'

'Every time things don't go right,' I say, 'You learn something. You and Ariane – you must be polymaths.'

We laugh. It's not amusing.

*

The game, the stakes – belong to Malek and to Ariane.

For me – it's boring. Uncertain, too. Work's like that, of course. You're paid an arbitrary sum, the prospects are obscure, and what you do – does it do harm? You're not asked to judge, and often if you do, they throw you out.

Activity is gratifying, paid work is mostly not.

'You're a loafer, Umar,' says Ariane, turning on me, severe and probing. 'A non-achiever. You expect people will pick you up, use you, throw you back ... a poor fish....'

'Take an example, Ariane,' I say. 'Think of my namesake.... I could do poetry, even astronomy. You can buy the book. Then there's advice to rulers: I'm an expert, not an original.'

'There's rulers,' says Ariane, 'And there's people who've been selected to sit on empty thrones.'

'Which do you hope to be?' I ask. 'You're not the bourgeoisie, you don't own, you don't control. You're brigands, sergeants in slave armies – people in the service, who aspire to run the show ...'

'If that is so,' she says. 'We're unstoppable. On the throne, there's always spendthrifts, simpletons, or losers. In the end, the system needs us to take over, and promote, exile, execute....'

I say. 'There's an Iranian movie. Two people, looking for a lost girl – you'd say they were intellectuals, though they don't do anything creative, nor use their heads. They drive in the mountains, to the villages, knock on doors, drink tea, motor over one-track roads. The girl stays lost, no one knows what's useful, and the rural people, helpful, crazy, bemused – they stay where they were. Two worlds, and something, someone, lost, an endless search, communication but no contact: incomprehension....'

'Who are you looking for, Umar?' she asks. 'I've not seen anything you've done, or you might do. No one's been lost but you.'

'No,' I say. 'I think it's all gone past. Me – I don't have a world, even a lonely one, to step back on to. I didn't come by spaceship, there's no ground control.'

'In the movie,' she says, 'no doubt there were some cows. This kind of rumination – it's passé, or else it's been confined to moos. Once, it was called *accidie.* You'd call it *Weltschmerz.* I was brought up to deal with big names when I met them, even if the people inside were small, aged like netsuke with tobacco juice. I'm a good fit, anywhere, with anyone.'

'There isn't much to say,' I say. 'There'll always be people like you and Malek.'

'Yes,' she says, 'We're eternal, indispensable. We drive the cart; the oxen pull. And some, like you, Umar, trudge on behind and pick up things that's fallen off the load.'

'It can't be about you and me,' I say. 'We're not even representatives of anything. It's the species – not up to it. Problems too big....'

'Biology?' she asks, 'Destiny? Those are the afterthoughts, not explanations. Come with us; or do some charity....'

'I don't want him, Ariane,' says Malek, loudly. 'He's a waste.'

'I'll drift,' I say. 'Don't consider me. Maybe I'll try doctoring....'

'He leads you on, Ariane,' says Malek. 'We want to do a deal, not rule anything or anyone.'

'All right,' I say, 'I've gone with you as far as possible. Let's end it here.'

And so we do.

*

If only there were ends. Funerals are made for that. Then too there's more, much more.

*

Ariane, months later, says, 'We haven't missed you, but I wondered....'

I'm not impressed.

She says, 'Malek had tough experiences you don't consider. A civil war. At night, I swear, he slips out his bones – there's three of us lie there – his spirit, and his bones, and me.'

'I know you think I'm bland,' I say. 'I had a close relationship once. It turned out a mistake.'

'I could have guessed.' she says. 'Sex is much smoother now. Just go against your nature – somebody must pay.'

'There was a death,' I say. 'No one understands those, I don't expect you to. Always unpredictable, always by chance. Of course – there is intention. It's mysterious, where it arises, where it leads.... Intention and the will – are they a challenge to my philosophy? Do they defy chance? Or do they arise, and perish, in the happenstance? Chance is ever-present, cause, result – but intention.... Is a challenge to my understanding, I agree. Intent to kill, even to kill oneself. A triumph of the will – or chaos? It seems quite inexplicable. And you can't bring luck in.'

We pause. Intention's not something she wants to hear about – in her case, intent is evident. Intention to defraud.

'This green stuff,' she goes on. 'Nature. It's all a fraud. It should be free, it's not: and you use precious stuff and can't just dump it, and you put the insects into cans and people gag.... All that – can't be right.'

I agree. It doesn't matter if I do.

'The Caucasus,' says Ariane. 'Is wonderful. Magical. But there's many sides, each can be more cruel than the next. I've lived with that, with Malek. Still, commerce is in our hearts.

'We live in France, we're not from there, we're usually somewhere else. My heart too; Provence is like that – not wanting to be where it is. People have wrong ideas about me,' and she ogles me, quite modestly.

'I don't want to be involved with you,' I say. 'Not you, not Malek.'

She ponders this, works it around her face, as if I've given her a caramel.

'I'm lonely, Umar,' she says. 'Business. Being in a gang – it seems a simple life, just making cash. It costs, Umar, believe me. Loneliness.'

'That's vague, Ariane,' I say. 'We're born alone, unless we're twins. The rest is up to you.'

I wish she'd go. She hovers, wants to stay, but has no reason to.

'The left, the right – it's all complicity and favours done,' she says, 'And each has their own mafia. Some go to jail, most don't. Jail changes you, Umar. Left, right – they don't.'

'Yours is a taking up of arms, Ariane....' I say, half joking. 'You sally forth! You don't have the faith, but you want conquest. You've doubts ... you want me round to tell you what is due to luck, and what is due to you, your cleverness.'

'Like they say,' she says, '"God will forgive us." I don't have the faith, but I know what goodness is. That's humility. You believe in luck, Umar. That's smart, but unavailing. Some animals are intelligent – even small birds. Pigs. But they're not intelligent enough to stop them being caged or eaten. Horses tried, and then gave up. Those races! The betting, and the fix! They couldn't beat the book. No one ever has. The rest run round in Africa until they're gunned down, or starve. Is that what you want, Umar? You think you're intelligent....'

'I believe in chance, not fortune, Ariane,' I say. 'It brings me nothing, and I don't pay.'

Of course, it's far-fetched, about the animals. Intelligence. It's exactly as she says: even with Malek the warrior, taking off his armour when he goes to bed. Spilling out his bones. You need intelligence to get around – but it doesn't mean the more you have, the more you last. Size and ferocity – those help too.

'Luck,' she says. 'I'll bet on that. Even if it leads to a cohabitation.'

'No, Ariane,' I say. 'I improvise, it's served me well. It doesn't give a resting place, but that is good – a goodness without faith. Resign yourself – there are no bets. It's chance. That's all.'

'Your life's a warning against paganism,' says Ariane. 'Chaos without, reflected in chaos within.'

'Your life, Ariane,' I respond. 'Is what happens when ambition seeks a ladder of belief. I'll mix the metaphors. Belief is a mistress who binds your knees so you can't run, you must fall down. She sleeps around with devils who promise to set you free....'

'Ah,' she says, 'For you, women mean just threatening sex? Poor poetic Umar!'

'My eyes and ears register everything perfectly,' I say. 'You can't "believe" in luck, Ariane: it doesn't care, it's absolutely neutral to "if you do" and "if you don't". It's not a basis for relationships ... you might try rolling dice, as that's the thing the poets do.'

'I didn't know that, Umar,' she says, wondering, her face turned up, the wrinkles smoothing with the tension. She looks quite beautiful, like when you see a lake, been there a million years – a breeze passes, and the water breathes it in, away its wrinkles, the tears come to you as you see it as it was, young, clean.

*

They say each person has a core that survives, more or less intact, or maybe ageing like a tree ... what happens in a life, the interludes of tragedy and comedy, pain and pleasure, fall on this tree like rain, wind, carvings, insect paths .... These are pricks and caresses. Like a sculptor working with a scalpel, they leave their grooves, worked surfaces, but nothing recognisable takes shape.... The you, the tree, the yew, perhaps ... survives: until one day, it falls, is burnt.

Ash to ashes.

I don't agree. There is no tree. There's tragedy and comedy, as if they importune you in the street. The unpredictable encounters make a script, a character, a text. Your breath turns the pages.... When it stops, the text, the gallimaufry of jumbled genres, a printer's pie – it terminates. It's archived, never read – maybe it's pulped or burnt.

*

'I'm desperate, Umar,' says Ariane. 'I wouldn't come to you, unless I needed your totality. Your devotion, your commitment. My cry, Umar! My howl! What I have, I'll give right back, but you must give me everything, and you'll receive a treasure in return, and more, much more....'

'I'm always desperate,' I say. 'Time! It swirls. Erodes – ticks away as sand grains falling.... But I don't ask, don't promise anything. Why your change of register, Ariane? You and Malek deny responsibilities – and yet you cause desperation, whether you have won or lost....'

'There's breaking rules, Umar,' she says. 'To change our lives. There's deals – in capital, in people on the move ... drugs, arms and medicines, the making peace and war, trading stuff and stealing it .... songs and messages, the preachermen, the bigots, rebels....

'The problem is, for me and Malek, and now with you, Umar ... we find the scene is full. It's terribly full. We're toads born in a hole that's closing fast, and up we struggle, a bejeweled and sacred knot, venomous – guardians of ourselves.... Doomed! Help us! Help us and yourself!'

'No,' I say. 'Absolutely and without appeal. Anyway – what is the plan?'

*

'The plan,' says Ariane, 'Is – to find a hole. Instead of digging one – find an empty space, and fill it. Don't try to build – find a used burrow, scuttle in....'

More fiddles, I think: what a bore.... Saving the world with fresh inventions – quite pathetic....

'I've been in error, Ariane,' I say. '"Luck" is the good side of chance. Chance has its bad side, what we call bad luck. I have misled you both....'

'It's academic, Umar,' says Ariane. 'We don't listen to you. It's your renunciation that stands out – your sacrifice. Your hedonism, your "waiting for what turns up...". Not sticking anywhere. It makes you seem holy. Not a fool, exactly.... An ascetic. Seeking neither pain, nor pleasure.... The right person to find the hole.... You live in one....'

I tell her, 'You organise the scam, or you expose it. Those are the choices. When you expose it, it leads to an enlargement. Everyone wants in, and paper profits rise. Every fraud involves a sale of certificates, with hope attached,' I say. 'Dead souls – the deal. Korobochka exposes Chichikov – grasps the real, the underlying value of the scheme....'

She interrupts, 'No, no, Umar. None of your Russian pals....'

I say, 'Forget the morality, everyone has lost it long ago; the reek of decadence, the rottenness – it's past. No one is interested in denunciations of sick worlds.... Besides, decadence is my star, my favourite refuge....'

'The hole, Umar,' says Ariane. 'Show us what is to fill it....'

'Dead souls,' I say, improvising. 'Souls don't fill a hole. The hole's for them. Spirits don't take up the space. The hole is full and empty. There'll be room for you.

'People dead, or never existed – false names and pseudonyms. Dead at sea; missing, in prison, in war, in camps. In flight, or not accounted for. Without papers, working alongside me, sex, cleaning, hiding, mining, rigging, peddling and pedalling. Listed in no census, no credits, not registered as subversives, as subsidised, as donors of their organs or their lives, not as displaced, not as underground nor floating in the water....

'The names – your asset. They're your workforce. They can be customers, backers, shareholders and sponsors, influencers, celebrities, anything you want – you'll never hear from them, they'll not complain.…

'They're the substance, the mystic flesh – a body to invest in, to organise, administer – attracting subsidies and fines: and loans, investments. You pay them – the absent dead. They don't collect. A payroll of specters....'

'It's old hat, Umar,' Ariane says. 'I've seen it written somewhere....'

I go on, 'A bank made cheap loans to pay debts that shortly would be repaid.... It got its money by borrowing, and issued bonds backed by those hypothetical repayments ... a Ponzi scheme.... It was a marvel, till it failed.

'What you do, Ariane, since the dead don't work, and economically they don't exist – is sell, exploit, give value to, the names ... as if they're working in the schemes you peddled, you and Malek, and which no one would promote. They must be paid, recruited, more and more. Dead – is safer, but the nameless live will do.

'So, the schemes they work on – they need more investment, and you pay with paper.... There's gigantic plans – bridges and mines, new cities, artificial islands, dams and lakes.... Everybody eating grass and worms, like corpses in the cemeteries. Experts and explorers, publicists and critics – all must be paid.... And you, dear Ariane, you are the blocked drain, the conduit where the money flows, and stops....

'You must get out, of course, before the end. You run; enjoy your cash.

'Not doing, stealing – you might give the humankinds a few years respite, a pause from digging, eating....

'Who knows? Others might really build the schemes you two hypothesised, and there'll be real souls working, being fired and falling under trucks.... A transformation, concrete labour making concrete.... In the end, it isn't names but time that's bought, and sold.'

'Of course,' I assure her. 'I want no part. Capitalism – hosts the big and little scams... But it's for you. It has been done before, it's tried – you win, if you get out before it fails. You must be prudent, leave before the end, which almost no one does.

'You needn't draw the lesson, a moral, about the world gone wrong. It's known: who cares, it makes no odds. It's an opinion; there's no conclusion, no intent, and no "now what?".

'If you can't do good, then make a fortune, Ariane. You want it so, and so – I am let out.

'It's a plot, with no need for chance or luck. The game is finding players who will play in it. Poker for suckers, not to play cards, but to sit silent on the chairs ... lay bare their cash.

'I want no money for the idea – it isn't mine....

'Just for my time, my remembering the ploy ... a small advance, Ariane? The scheme is harmless, and it works, it's working everywhere....

'Go in peace. The dead can't fight, or threaten war, burn your house, or rape you or your friends ... and ... you can't hurt the dead. You try to have them not hurt you.'

*

Ariane's delighted, though of course – it's different ways of selling nothing.

I get a pittance for my rhetoric. Poetry, if you can manage it, ought to let you travel faster, further – but there's no promise, and no pay.

*

Chance will be my guide.

About the author

John Fraser lives near Rome. Previously, he worked in England and Canada.